AN HONOURABLE WAGER

Lizzie lives a simple life . . . until Jack moves in next door, invading her privacy, and Paul, interested in her lifestyle, wants her to write about it for his newspaper. When Paul bets she can't be self-sufficient for a year, Lizzie takes the wager — in return for a charitable donation to the hospital that has helped her ill niece. But then the deal proves more challenging than she'd expected and she comes to realise just how welcome Jack's presence is . . .

SARAH SWATRIDGE

◆

AN HONOURABLE WAGER

Complete and Unabridged

LINFORD
Leicester

First published in Great Britain in 2009

First Linford Edition
published 2010

British Library CIP Data

Swatridge, Sarah.
    An honourable wager.- -
    (Linford romance library)
    1. Self-reliant living- -Fiction. 2. Wagers- -
    Fiction. 3. Neighbors- -Fiction. 4. Love stories.
    5. Large type books.
    I. Title II. Series
    823.9'2–dc22

    ISBN 978–1–44480–075–3

Published by
F. A. Thorpe (Publishing)
Anstey, Leicestershire

Set by Words & Graphics Ltd.
Anstey, Leicestershire
Printed and bound in Great Britain by
T. J. International Ltd., Padstow, Cornwall

This book is printed on acid-free paper

1

Lizzie was in her garden weeding. 'Hello, Auntie Liz!' called Fiona cheerfully, as she opened the picket gate and carefully closed it after her, despite her mother and little brother being only a little way behind. Once, she had left it open, and the goats had escaped. It had taken ages to round them up again and, although it had been fun, Fiona had learnt her lesson.

'Can you come to tea?' Fiona asked. 'I'm bursting with things to tell you,' said the eight-year-old.

'Can't you tell me now?' asked Lizzie as she took off her gardening gloves and gave Fiona a big hug. 'I bet it's that you've grown?' Fiona shook her head. 'Lost a tooth?'

The picket gate squeaked and an elegant young woman walked in wearing high heels. 'I do wish you'd get a phone, or at least let us buy you a mobile. It's ridiculous having to traipse over here just to give you a quick message,' Sally sighed as she tried to grab hold of Sidney's hand. He was too quick and was soon off exploring the large garden. 'I'm sorry, I hope he won't trample on anything . . . edible.'

'Don't worry about him,' reassured Lizzie. She stood up and stretched. She ached from all the weeding. 'What's the message?'

'We want you to come to tea!' interrupted Fiona. 'Today. It has to be today.'

'Darling,' Sally soothed, 'Auntie Liz may be busy today.'

Lizzie looked around her. There were always things to do in her garden or in the kitchen. 'Tea today would be lovely. It will save me having to cook later on. When do you want me?'

'Now!' said Fiona excitedly.

'You'll have to give me a little while to tidy up, have a wash and put the chickens to bed so that nasty Mr Fox won't get them.'

'I'll help!' offered Fiona.

'She's welcome to give me a hand and we'll catch you up in about half an hour.' Lizzie looked at her sister-in-law and added, 'If that's OK?'

'Stay,' said Sidney. He was a child of few words. Lizzie bent down to give her nephew a hug.

'If you can manage?' asked Sally haughtily. She was fifteen years younger than Lizzie, but, because she was a married woman with a family, she classed herself as superior.

'Sally,' said Lizzie gently. 'I used to be a primary school teacher, I'm sure I'll be able to manage my niece and nephew.' Lizzie smiled contentedly, holding their hands. 'Is there anything you'd like me to bring?'

'Could I have some mint, please? Just a little, Richard's home tomorrow and I'm hoping to welcome him back with a dinner party. I'm doing a fruit punch. I think it's one of your recipes.'

'Mint's no problem, but I thought I'd

given you a plant only a short while ago.'

Sally looked down toward her feet. 'You're always giving me plants. I don't think it was mint. I really can't tell the difference. They all look green to me.'

'It was mint. I remember the smell, but it's dead now,' said Fiona. 'Mummy forgot to water it.'

'You know what I'm like with plants!' laughed Sally.

'Never mind, I've got loads, it spreads like anything. Is it OK if I let the children choose which type you want — peppermint, spearmint, apple mint?'

'Any sort will be lovely. I'll see you all in about half-an-hour.' Sally paused. 'And Liz, don't let them get too dirty.'

It didn't take long to round up the chickens and put them in their coop. It was easier with someone to help.

Sidney gave the goats fresh water and Fiona fed them a bit of hay while Lizzie freshened up.

As she was in her bedroom brushing

her long dark hair tinged with grey, she noticed a stranger in the garden next door. The house had been empty for years and Lizzie wondered how safe it was inside. Quickly she twisted her hair up into a knot on the back of her head and ran downstairs to be with the children.

She let them pick a variety of mints from her herb garden and put them in a jam jar with a little water. As they were doing so, the tall, silver-haired stranger she had seen from her bedroom window appeared at the garden fence.

'Can I help?' Lizzie asked.

'Do you know where I can get a key?' he asked. His voice was mellow and he smiled kindly at the children. Laugh lines showed near his eyes and Lizzie couldn't help smiling back.

'You can ask at the farmhouse along the lane, but be careful in there. I don't know how safe it is. It's been derelict for years.'

'Thanks for your help Mrs . . . '

'Elliot, Lizzie.' She watched him go

down the lane and turn into the farm track. 'Come on then, let's go and have some tea.'

It was only a short walk to her brother's house where he lived with his wife, Sally, and their two children, Fiona and Sidney, and yet there was such a sharp contrast.

'It's like time travel,' said Fiona.

'Pardon?'

'We go back in time to your cottage and forward to our house. Mummy calls it the real world.'

'Doesn't she think I live in the real world too?' asked Lizzie.

'No, she's always telling Daddy you live in the dark ages. She gets really cross sometimes.' Lizzie felt it was time to change the subject before Fiona said too much.

'Which do you like best?' asked Lizzie. Fiona thought for a while.

'Both. I love going back in time but I couldn't live without TV.'

'And what about you, Sidney?' asked Lizzie in a quiet voice.

'Paddy and Ginty,' he said simply.

'I know you like the goats. Paddy was really naughty the other day. He managed to get free and nibbled all my clean washing!'

They came to the end of the grass track that led down to Lizzie's cottage. Now there was a new road which led to a recently built, and very expensive, housing estate. It looked very sparse to Lizzie but she told herself it would look better once the trees and shrubs matured.

Lizzie couldn't help looking up the farm path where she had directed the stranger. There was no sign of him, but Lizzie could see him clearly in her mind.

Sally's new people carrier sat on the drive leading up to the double garage. The garden was mainly grass, with a few rose bushes in a flower bed.

Fiona ran up to the front door and hammered on it calling, 'We're home!'

Sally opened the door to let them in. the children dutifully removed their shoes and left them at the door. Lizzie slipped off her shoes too for fear of upsetting Sally if she were to get a dirty mark on the cream coloured carpet.

'Tea's nearly ready. Why don't you go in the lounge for a few minutes?'

Lizzie sat on the creamy leather sofa with a child on each side. Fiona got out her school reading book and read to them.

'Now it's your turn to read to us,' announced Fiona when she'd finished her school book.

'Tea's ready. Wash your hands and come and sit up.'

The table was covered with healthy, but shop bought food. Sally said she didn't have time to cook.

'Look!' said Fiona proudly waving a piece of paper in the air. 'We made a newspaper at school and the real editor came in from The Chronicle and said it was very good.'

'That's excellent,' said Lizzie. 'Which bit did you do?'

'Don't worry about that now. It's tea

time,' reminded Sally. Fiona ignored her mother and found the page she was looking for.

'But that's why I wanted Auntie Liz over!' explained Fiona. 'I wrote this article all about you and your farm.'

'It's not really a farm. I only have a few animals. The farm's next door.'

'Well anyway. I said how it was just like going back into olden times and how clever you were, but do you know what?' Fiona's voice sounded indignant.

'What?' asked Lizzie as she politely took a sandwich.

'The editor said it was a good story but in a real newspaper they don't have fiction, just fact. I told him he didn't know what he was talking about.'

'I hope you didn't,' interrupted Sally with a stern look.

'I wasn't rude, but I told him it was all true and if he didn't believe me he should come and see for himself!'

'And what did he say to that?' asked Lizzie.

'He said he'd love to and he would bring a photographer,' Fiona paused with her sandwich in one hand.

'A photographer's coming to me?' said Lizzie. 'I'll have to shampoo the goats!'

'I think so, but I'm not sure, Sophie was poking me in the back because she wanted to show the editor her picture.'

'I'm sure they won't just turn up,' began Lizzie. 'This tea is lovely. You'll have to come to me next time, especially if your dad's home.'

'Richard's due home at the weekend, but we'll be very busy.'

'Oh well, do let me know if I can babysit or anything.'

'Actually,' said Sally, 'I was hoping you might do me a table arrangement for the dinner party on Saturday night?'

'Certainly. I love working with flowers. What colour do you want?'

'I've got ivory napkins . . . '

'How about using those beautiful red roses you've got in the front garden?'

'Good idea.'

'It'll be easier if I come round on Saturday and do it here. Perhaps I can have a few minutes with Richard?'

'Daddy,' said Sydney and Fiona lent over and gave him a sisterly kiss.

It was beginning to get dark by the time Lizzie walked up the lane on her way home. The children had wanted one story after another and then she had helped Sally choose the menu for Saturday.

Lizzie slowed as she neared her home. She thought she'd seen a shadowy figure in the garden. As she watched, she saw something move. Suddenly it dawned on Lizzie that Paddy the goat might have somehow managed to get out of his field and be free to roam around the vegetables patch.

Lizzie ran through the picket gate and headed blindly toward the small paddock where the goats grazed. She let out a gasp as she realised she was not alone.

'I didn't mean to startle you,' a man's

voice said. Lizzie recognised the mellow tones of the strange man who'd been hanging around earlier.

'What are you doing in my garden?' she demanded.

'I thought I heard a noise,' he said. 'It sounded like an animal.'

'I keep animals,' said Lizzie shortly.

'It sounded in pain,' he explained. 'I didn't mean any harm, I was just concerned.'

'Well, it's fine now. I'm home, you can go and I'd be grateful if you didn't trespass on my property in future!'

He brushed past her as he made for the path on his way out of the garden.

The handsome stranger had not reached the gate when they both heard a strangled cry. He turned and made his way back to Lizzie's side. He carried a torch which he flashed around in the direction the noise had come from.

'My chickens!' cried Lizzie as she ran towards the little hen house. She clapped and waved her arms around. In the torchlight they saw the unmistakeable red fur of a fox. 'Shoo!' called Lizzie. The man ran forward shouting and the fox disappeared.

'Ah!' yelped the man as he jumped up in the air and tripped over something. He fell back down to the ground and yelled out in agony.

Lizzie turned round and saw Paddy with a piece of cloth in his mouth. 'What have you got there?' she asked as she approached the goat. He seemed to think it was a game and ran off.

'What was that?' said a voice from the ground.

Lizzie offered him her hand to help him up. 'I'm sorry, that's Paddy, my goat. He's always seen himself as a sort of guard dog. He's harmless but . . .' before Lizzie could finish the sentence, McGinty had barged into her and sent her flying. She landed on top of the strange man.

'Oh, I'm so sorry,' she said trying to pick herself up.

'Here,' said the man, 'let me give you a hand,' He rose to his feet and easily helped her up again.

'Paddy,' called Lizzie in a coaxing voice and obediently he walked over to her and held up his chin to be tickled. Lizzie stroked him with one hand and grabbed his collar with the other. 'I'll take him back to his pen and get another torch so we can check that the chickens are OK.'

'I'll try and catch the other one,' the man suggested but his voice did not sound confident.

It didn't take long for Lizzie to return Paddy to his pen and to fetch a torch. She easily caught McGinty who recognised her voice. As soon as she too was shut up with Paddy for the night, they went to inspect the hen house for damage.

'I think he was just sniffing around,' said the man. 'There's no sign of a break in.' Lizzie double checked, but had to agree that the chicken wire was still intact.

'Thank you for your help,' she said quietly, now feeling embarrassed, knowing that he had just been trying to help.

'I suppose I'd better go and clean up,' he said.

'You're not living next door are you?' asked Lizzie.

'No. It needs too much doing to it. I'm staying at the pub in the village. I was just out for a walk. It's beautiful round here.'

'It is,' agreed Lizzie. 'Look, why don't you come in and wash your hands. Do you want a cup of tea?'

'I won't say no,' he paused as Lizzie reached her front door. 'I'm Jack, by the way.' He held out his hand and then they both laughed as in the light of Lizzie's cottage they realised just how dirty they both were. 'On second thoughts, I'll go back to the pub and have a bath. Will you be all right now?'

'I'll be fine,' Lizzie smiled at the stranger. Even with his hair ruffled up and a muddy face he was still dazzlingly handsome. 'Thanks again for your help,' she called as he disappeared down the dark lane.

The following day Lizzie was up

early. She fed the chickens and let the goats into the small field to graze. She couldn't see any damage but tightened up the hinges on the gate of the goat pen.

While it was still early Lizzie wandered round her garden snipping here and there at a selection of leafy foliage ready to condition in water for making her sister-in-law's arrangement that evening.

The day passed rapidly with weeding and planting and Lizzie lost all track of time. Once or twice during the day she had caught herself day dreaming about the silver-haired man called Jack who had come to her rescue.

Lizzie rarely let herself dwell on how things might have been. She had thrown herself into her career as a teacher and was kept so busy she never had time for a social life. She was happy. She loved her job and was rewarded by feeling loved by all she taught. It was a small village school in those days and everyone knew everyone in the village. The atmosphere was lovely. Lizzie felt the whole community was her family.

Then her mother passed away shortly followed by her father, and Richard moved abroad to work. By the time he returned five years later having met and married Sally, the village had changed beyond recognition.

Two farms had been sold and hundreds of houses had been built. The village school was no longer large enough to cater for the growing population. It was replaced by a huge modern school on the other side of the village.

Lizzie recalled the day she'd returned from the solicitor's office having received her share of her parents' estate. She should have been glad to be a wealthy woman but she'd looked in the mirror and just saw a middle aged woman with bags under her eyes and a pasty complexion.

It wasn't long after, that she bought the dilapidated old cottage and refurbished it. The more time she spent making the house comfortable and taming the large plot, the more she realised how much she enjoyed the outdoor life. Her complexion improved but there were too many changes at the new school that Lizzie didn't care for, and soon she decided to take early retirement at 50. She had shut herself away and tried to live in harmony with nature.

'Thank God you've arrived!' said Sally. 'I was beginning to get worried that I wouldn't have a table decoration for this evening.'

Lizzie smiled at her sister-in-law. 'You knew I wouldn't let you down. I just got carried away in the garden and forgot the time.' Lizzie hugged her niece, nephew and then her brother as he came to greet her as she arranged the things round her in the kitchen.

As Lizzie worked with the flowers, Fiona sat quietly and watched. It didn't take long before she'd transformed individual flowers into a beautiful table decoration.

'That's lovely,' said Sally as she

whisked it off into the dining-room.

Lizzie sipped her tea and was pleased to find herself alone with her brother.

'Richard,' she said, 'I hope you don't think I'm interfering, but I am concerned about Sidney. He hardly says a word and when he does speak, he doesn't say a whole sentence. He's nearly five and he'll be starting school before you know it.'

'Sally has taken him to the doctor. He just said that Fiona's such a chatterbox, he doesn't get a chance to speak. Don't worry.'

At that moment Sally came back into the room and reminded Richard that he only had half an hour before their guests arrived and he had to get changed and be ready to serve the welcome drink.

'I'll talk to you over dinner,' said Richard to Lizzie.

'She's not staying,' said Sally as though Lizzie was just a servant bought in for her floristry skills.

'Have you eaten?' Richard asked Lizzie.

'Not yet, I've been in the garden all day, but it's no problem, I can get something when I get home. I'll just stay and put the children to bed for you and then slip off.'

The doorbell rang. Sally went pale and looked at the clock.

'Quick, Richard, go and get changed!' she ordered.

'Paul!' said Sally loudly to let Richard, and the whole household know that their guests had started to arrive. 'How lovely to see you! Do come in. Richard will be down in a moment. He'll get you a drink.'

As Paul entered, taking off his coat, Fiona rushed passed her mum and into the kitchen where Lizzie was tidying up her things.

'Auntie Liz! It's him!'

Lizzie looked up. 'Who?'

'The man who said my article about you was a story!' Fiona was pulling on her hand and dragged her through to the lounge where Sally was making small talk with their guest.

As Fiona entered with Lizzie, Richard came through the opposite door and shook hands with Paul. Lizzie couldn't conceal a gasp as she looked at the man. He reminded her of the man who'd been in her garden but she couldn't be sure.

'This is Lizzie, my sister,' said Richard. The man offered his hand but made no sign of recognising her. They briefly shook hands.

'This is my auntie,' announced Fiona. 'The one who lives in the past. Honest. You ask her!'

'Lizzie, would you mind taking Fiona up to bed?' asked Sally coolly.

'It's not my bedtime!' argued Fiona. 'Besides, Sidney's still up.'

'Come along with me and we'll find Sidney,' suggested Lizzie still holding Fiona's hand.

'So do you believe me now?' asked Fiona.

The man smiled down at Fiona. It

was a shallow smile. 'I tell you what, you go off to bed like a good little girl and I'll talk to your auntie about her lifestyle.'

Fiona tried to stand her ground but Sidney had found a frog in the garden and wanted everyone to come and see.

'I'll lay another place,' said Sally to herself as everyone else went to inspect the frog.

2

'I understand you're self-sufficient,' said Paul as they all sat down to dinner having got the children settled in bed.

'I'm not really self-sufficient,' admitted Lizzie. 'I just live very simply.'

Paul smiled a rather smug smile. Lizzie could still see why he reminded her of Jack, but where as she felt comfortable in his company, this man made her feel defensive.

'I didn't think she was telling the truth,' said Paul as he helped himself to a bread roll and dipped it in his soup.

'Are you referring to Fiona's article in the school newspaper?' asked Lizzie.

'Her story,' corrected Paul. 'It was pure fiction.'

'Actually, what she wrote was perfectly true. I do live off the land and even though I'm not totally self-sufficient, I could be if I needed to.'

Paul laughed mockingly. 'No-one could be self-sufficient in this day and age. We're all dependent on computers and high tech. Aren't we Richard?'

'Well,' began Richard looking a bit awkward. 'I agree, most people would find it extremely difficult to give up things like television and phones, but you've not met my sister before.'

The other guests were equally amazed that Lizzie didn't have a television or a phone.

'She doesn't even have a dishwasher or an electric kettle!' said Sally with a deep sigh.

'There's only me, so I don't have much washing up and I have a gas hob which heats the kettle.'

'You must have a washing machine and tumble drier though?' said one of the guests. Liz shook her head.

'I hand wash most things and Sally insists on doing my sheets and towels. It's very good of her.'

'It's so inconvenient though,' said Sally. 'The amount of times I've had to go over to Milkmaid's Cottage just to ask if she can baby-sit or to let her know Richard's flying off again. I've even offered to buy her a phone, but she won't hear of it.'

'So, do you sneak round here to watch the soap operas?' asked Paul leaning forward and poking fun at Lizzie.

'You don't understand. I choose to live a simple life. I'm not punishing myself. I can afford all these things. I just don't feel I need them.'

'More wine?' asked Richard as he could see tensions rising.

'I'm willing to bet you a fantastic holiday anywhere in the world that you couldn't live without all mod cons for a week!'

Sally collected up the soup bowls. 'Lizzie's never had any mod cons for as long as I can remember.'

'This would make a good story. If you can really do it for a week, where would you go on holiday? I can just see this on the front page . . . I'm sure donations would come in just to buy you a telly.'

'Can we change the subject? No-one would be interested in whether I've got a TV or not.'

'Don't you believe it! People love to read human-interest stories. How about a world tour . . . if you can do it for a month? I bet you can't.'

'Can I help you in the kitchen?' asked Lizzie ignoring Paul's latest offer and following her sister-in-law out of the dining room.

'A thousand pounds if we can do a story on you living without a TV for a month. You look like a person who likes a challenge.'

Lizzie put down the plates she was carrying and looked straight at Paul. Slowly and clearly she said, 'For the last time, I am not interested!' There was a moment's silence and then Lizzie said quietly to her hosts, 'Would you mind awfully if I made a move? I really ought to check on the chickens, I've had a fox round recently and I want to make sure they're safe.'

The following Monday, Lizzie collected

Fiona from school as Sally had taken Sidney out for the day. Lizzie walked past the public house in the village where Jack had told her he was staying. Lizzie couldn't help looking into the courtyard to see if he was there, but there was no sign of him.

Lizzie wondered why she was disappointed. He was nothing to her and only reminded her, with annoyance, of the arrogant newspaper editor.

By the time they reached Fiona's home, Sally and Sidney were back from their day trip to the zoo.

'I've got you this,' said Sally passing Lizzie a small box with a picture of a mobile phone on it.

'Don't you start,' said Lizzie handing back the box.

'Please,' begged Sally. 'Just for emergencies. What if I broke down and couldn't collect Fiona from school, or if I had an accident?'

'OK. If you insist.' agreed Lizzie seeing the sense in what her sister-in-law was saying. Rather luckily, as it turned out . . .

A few days later, Lizzie was feeling pleased with herself. She had put straw under the strawberries, thinned out the carrots and weeded round the onions and garlic, and it was still early in the day. She had just stopped for a break when a friendly voice called 'Hello!'. It was Jack. He looked even more handsome in the daylight. He was tall, probably at least six foot but despite that he didn't appear to stoop. His hair was mainly silver but dusted with dark strands from the past.

The most dazzling thing about him, were his eyes. They were a beautiful blue, but it wasn't so much the colour and the depth, but the way he looked. He seemed to look right into her, not in an unkind way. It was a way that showed he was interested in what she had to say, a genuine interest.

'This is an impressive plot,' he said.

'Thank you,' said Lizzie straightening herself up and rubbing her back.

'Is that your phone?' he asked.

Lizzie looked puzzled and then

mumbled an apology before running into the house to look for the phone. She couldn't remember exactly where she'd left it, but was able to track it down because of the noise it made.

'Hello?'

'What took you so long?' asked Sally. 'Fiona's got a really bad stomach ache. Can you come and take Sidney to nursery, so I can be here for the doctor?'

'No problem,' said Lizzie. 'What time's your appointment?'

'I've had to call the doctor out, she's doubled over in pain and there's no way I could get her to the surgery.'

'I'll come straight away,' said Lizzie. She quickly washed her hands and ran her fingers through her hair.

Jack had gone by the time she locked up her front door and hurried over to her sister-in-law's.

Fiona was obviously in a lot of pain. She clutched her stomach and said she felt sick.

'She hardly ate anything yesterday or

the day before. She's just slept and slept.'

'She's had tummy aches before,' said Lizzie as she stroked Fiona's forehead.

'This is much worse,' said Sally with a tremble in her voice.

'I'll take Sidney to nursery. Do you want anything from the chemist, while I'm out?'

'I'd better wait and see what the doctor says.' Sally gave Sidney a hug and kissed him goodbye. 'You be good for Auntie Lizzie.'

Liz explained to the nursery staff why Sidney was a bit late. 'I don't suppose he would tell you himself that Fiona wasn't very well.'

'He doesn't say much,' said the nursery nurse with a smile, 'except when he's playing. You should hear him chatter away when he's got the farm to himself. He makes all the animal noises and the farmer tells his wife not to leave the gate open otherwise the goats will get out or the fox will get in and scare the chickens.'

'I'm glad to hear that he does talk. I was getting very worried about him.'

'So were we, but when we actually observed him and realised he can talk, we were relieved. He just chooses not to talk most of the time — unlike Fiona who never stopped,' laughed the nursery nurse. 'Is she still like that?'

'She does talk, although she was very quiet this morning. I do hope she'll be OK. It may be me who collects Sidney, depending how Fiona is.'

Liz called in on an old lady in the village and chatted for a little while. Liz did a little shopping for her and then walked home. She called in on her sister-in-law on her way back.

The car was in the drive, but there was no one in. Lizzie had a key and let herself in. She found a hurriedly written note on the kitchen table. The doctor had called an ambulance and Fiona had been taken into hospital. Sally had gone with her.

Liz checked her watch. She just had time to nip home and do a few jobs before she would have to collect Sidney from nursery.

On the way back from collecting him they called into a newsagent and together they chose a *Get Well Soon* card for Fiona and bought her a comic to read.

'Would you like to come and help me at Milkmaid's Cottage, until we hear from Mummy how Fiona is?'

'Ginty,' said Sydney in response.

'Yes, let's go and see how McGinty is. You can feed her some hay while I milk her.'

The afternoon went quickly. They collected the eggs, milked McGinty the goat and picked peas.

'Pop!' said Sidney as Lizzie showed him how to shell the peas into a small bowl.

'Do you want to taste one? They are good to eat, even before they're cooked.' She popped one in her mouth and then Sidney did the same.

They were distracted by the noise of a car. Milkmaid's Cottage was situated on a grass track. The only vehicle that ever ventured as far as the two cottages was a tractor, but today a bright red Jaguar was heading up the track toward them.

Lizzie's first thought, on seeing the man at the wheel, was that it was Jack, but when he stopped and slammed the door shut, she was disappointed to see it was the rude man from the newspaper.

For a moment Lizzie wondered why it bothered her. She couldn't explain why she felt disappointed. Neither man meant anything to her, but out of the two of them, she would much rather pass the time of day with Jack, who readily admitted he loved the country-side.

'Good!' declared the newspaperman. 'Glad I caught you in. I've brought a photographer.' As he was talking, he was looking up at her roof. 'No aerial,' he said to the photographer who snapped a shot.

'What are you doing?' asked Lizzie. 'I

have no objection with you seeing for yourself that Fiona and I were telling the truth, but there's no need to photograph it.'

'OK, Dave,' said Paul the editor. The photographer lowered his camera, but he didn't put it away. 'I must say you drive a hard deal.'

'There is no deal. I just want to prove a point and then you can go,' said Lizzie standing up. She showed Paul and Dave the photographer her small home. There was no TV or electric fire but there was an impressive woodpile outside the front door under a small shelter, ready for the winter. To the side of the house were a couple of Calor Gas bottles.

'We don't have mains gas up here,' she explained. 'I do have electricity although it's not very reliable.'

The house itself was sparse. In the kitchen was a small wooden table with four wooden chairs and a further rocking chair near the hearth.

The other downstairs room had bare

floorboards, a wooden dresser with a few pieces of china on display and a spinning wheel in the centre of the room.

'Sally and Richard gave it to me for Christmas and I have tried to collect some of the goat hair, but they're not Angoras. Sally means well and she's very generous but . . . '

'She's a townie,' said Paul and for the first time, Liz had to agree with him. 'Can we just see upstairs?' he asked but was on his way up the narrow wooden stairs before she could stop him.

There were two rooms upstairs, originally two bedrooms but when she had bought the cottage she had the smallest bedroom converted into an indoor bathroom. It was still very small, but was all she needed, with a simple white cast iron bath with a shower attachment, and a toilet.

'Only one toothbrush?' asked the photographer.

'I only need one,' explained Lizzie bristling as the two men looked around her bathroom for signs of twenty-first century life.

'Toilet rolls aren't very medieval?' sneered Paul and wrote something else down on his notepad.

'I told you before, I choose a simple life. I could use newspaper if I wanted, but I don't want to.'

'Hey Paul, come and look at this,' called the photographer from her bedroom. Paul wasted no time in darting across the hall, no doubt hoping he'd find a portable TV.

'What?' he asked looking at the sparsely decorated room.

'A single bed . . . '

At that moment the mobile phone rang again and, although Lizzie was reluctant to leave them in her room, she rushed down to the phone, knowing it would be Sally.

'I don't suppose you get your rubbish collected up here either?' asked the photographer when he came downstairs and Liz had finished talking to her sister-in-law.

'I recycle everything — either the goats eat it or it goes in the compost.'

'Very organic,' said Paul making a note of something. 'Green issues are very popular these days.'

'I told you . . . ' began Lizzie again.

'And what's this little lad doing here?' Before Lizzie could intervene, the photographer had snapped a shot of four-year-old Sidney shelling peas on the back step. 'That'll look good in sepia.'

'Enough!' said Lizzie. 'You've looked round, now off you go, and leave me alone.'

'Don't be too hasty,' said Paul reaching into his jacket pocket and pulling out his business card. 'Two thousand quid for a regular little story on this place — you know the kind of thing, living The Good Life, organic, healthy eating and all that, and then in the winter how you manage to keep warm, etc., etc. Must be very cosy in that little bed of yours.'

Lizzie could feel herself blushing and

was glad when Sidney distracted her by handing her the bowl of shelled peas.

'Fee?' he asked knowing that she'd been talking on the phone to his mum about his big sister.

'Fiona's much better. The doctor gave her some medicine and she's back home,' said Lizzie quietly to Sidney. Then she stood as tall as her five foot two body would let her and said, 'And these gentlemen are just going so we can take you home to see how she is.'

'Little girl not very well?' asked Paul who seemed very good at picking up anything and making it seem like it might make a good front page story.

'She's fine now, so it's old news. Let me show you out,' said Lizzie showing them the door.

As the two men brushed passed Lizzie, Paul squeezed his business card into her hand. 'Think about my offer. Dave here will tell you, I'm always open to new ideas and suggestions!' He looked her up and down, and she was sure he licked his lips.

His face changed and he suddenly looked menacingly serious. 'People don't mess with me, you know. I just want you to understand, when we shake on the deal, which we will because I always get my way, I'll keep my part and pay up, but ONLY if you stick to your side of the bargain. I won't be cheated on. No one, absolutely no one, cheats on me.' He spat out the last few words and then left.

Liz stood frozen to the spot and it was only the noise of the Jaguar's wheels spinning on the dry soil that seemed to bring her to her senses.

'Nasty man!' she said mainly to herself, but Sidney nodded.

'Fee,' he said.

'Good idea. Let's pack up and go and see how she is.'

Fiona was lying on the sofa watching TV. She had colour in her cheeks and looked very comfortable and relaxed. Sidney gave her the comic and card and snuggled up next to her to watch the programme.

'I could have hit him!' said Sally as she made herself and Lizzie a cup of tea in the kitchen. 'They kept us waiting for ages. One doctor would say it was her appendix, then another said it was too high. They kept poking her and prodding her and making her cry. Then ... ' Sally plonked the teapot down with a thud, 'Then, after she'd had a little sleep, she woke up feeling fine and they sent us home.'

'Did they say what they thought it was?' asked Lizzie surprised by what Sally was telling her.

'They said it was all in her mind, probably for attention because her daddy is away again and maybe because she's jealous of the attention Sidney gets!'

'But she looked as though she was in real pain.'

'That's because she was,' declared Sally, still seething. 'I know she does miss her dad, but he's often away and he calls every evening to chat to her and wish her a goodnight.'

They took their teacups into the lounge to check on the children. They were cuddled up together engrossed in the telly.

'Not much sibling rivalry there,' said Sally. 'Richard was livid when I rang him, but he told me not to worry. The main thing is that she's OK and it was nothing serious.'

'He's right of course,' agreed Lizzie. 'What's that?'

'Probably a text,' said Sally picking up Lizzie's phone and handing it to her.

'But you're the only one with my number,' said Lizzie looking puzzled. She looked at the screen and sighed. 'I wish he'd leave me alone!'

'Who?' asked Sally showing an interest.

'That awful man from the paper. He came round to check up on me that I really don't have a TV. What it's got to do with him, I really don't know, but he still doesn't seem to believe that I don't secretly nip round here to watch a film or send an e-mail.'

'He is taking quite an interest in you,' said Sally with a smile. 'I don't know him very well, but Richard's met him at the golf club a couple of times. I think his wife left him recently and he's really cut up. I felt a bit sorry for him, that's why I invited him for dinner,' Sally paused, 'Maybe he's over his relationship now . . . '

'I just wish he'd leave me alone,' said Lizzie finishing her cup of tea.

'You would say he was handsome though, wouldn't you?'

'Looks aren't everything!' said Lizzie switching off her phone and chucking it into her bag.

3

Lizzie saw the photographer from her bedroom window. She raced down the stairs and marched into the front garden. She just managed to stop herself when she realised that it was a different man, not the newspaper photographer but a man in a fluorescent jacket and a camera on a tripod.

The man showed her his ID card. 'I'm just doing a surveyor's report on your neighbour's property, so I shouldn't get in your way.'

'But it's been empty for years . . . ' began Lizzie. It suddenly dawned on her that she didn't know who the adjoining property belonged to. At one time she had had thoughts of buying it herself and knocking the two cottages into one, but she didn't need more room and had talked herself out of it because it would have just been more for her to keep clean and tidy. She now wondered if she had made the right decision.

'I'm just about to put the kettle on,' said Lizzie in a friendly way. 'Shall I make you a cup of tea?'

'I wouldn't say no,' said the surveyor.

Lizzie made a point of taking her tea cup out with her when she took the gentleman his hot drink. She was determined to find out what she could about the property next door, the work that needed doing to it and who was the true owner.

'It's a good sound property,' said the man, 'shame it's been left, but it won't take long to put right. It just needs a good clean and a lick of paint. Of course it would benefit from a new kitchen and bathroom, but it looks as though the windows were done about the same time as yours and it's got no major problems.' The man finished his tea and put the cup back on the tray. 'Of course there is the matter of the garden . . . '

'What's wrong with the garden?' asked Liz genuinely worried. The man laughed and held up his hands.

'Look at it! It'll take years to tame and to be a patch on yours. You must spend all day in your garden and is that field at the back yours too?'

'No, but the farmer isn't using it at the moment, so he lets me graze my goats.' Lizzie thought of the times she had thought about letting her goats lose on the land next door, thinking that no one would mind. Now she was pleased that the farmer had been good to her and she had not felt she needed to let them graze anywhere else.

'I bought my cottage from the farm. It's called Milkmaid's Cottage because years ago these were both farm workers' homes. Next door is called Mulberry Cottage because of the Mulberry tree in the front.'

'Well I must be getting on,' said the man, 'thanks for the tea.'

'So, what happens now?' pressed Lizzie. 'You'll presumably hand your report over to . . . '

'Sorry, love, I've done my bit, it's not up to me what happens next.'

Lizzie watched as the man walked down the track to where he'd left his van. She watched him get in and drive slowly away. She tried to concentrate on what she ought to be doing, but could not help wondering what was going to happen to the other half of her home and what effect it may or may not have on her.

On the spur of the moment, she grabbed a jacket and pulled the front door to. With purposeful strides she marched off toward the farmhouse.

'Hello, Lizzie,' greeted Mrs Marshall. 'You're looking well. What can I do for you?'

'I'm fine thank you, Mrs Marshall. Is your husband about?'

'He's up on Bull Field if you want him. Is there a problem?'

'Do you know who owns Mulberry Cottage?' asked Lizzie coming straight out with it.

'Sad tale that,' said Mrs Marshall. 'Poor Mr Curtis. Some reckons the place is jinxed, but I say that's all stuff and nonsense.' She paused, 'Why are you asking, it's a bit early for mulberries even with this climate change.'

Lizzie laughed, 'I'm not after the mulberries, at least not until they're ripe. It's just I've seen a lot of people looking around the place lately, one was in the garden and he asked about where he could get the keys, then today there was a surveyor taking photos and writing up a report on the place. I just wondered if I am likely to be getting new neighbours.'

'You're right, someone did come and ask for the keys. I sent him to Mr Curtis in town. To be honest, I think we do have the keys hanging up in the office but I didn't want to get involved.' Mrs Marshall folded her arms over her ample chest. 'Our *pick your own* opens up next week for the season. Is there anything I can interest you in? How are your crops doing?'

'So far, so good. The strawberries are looking healthy and I've had a lot of flowers on the raspberries, we just need a bit more sunshine and it should be a good harvest. I will let Sally, my sister-in-law, know you're open. She may want to bring the children over to pick some fruit.'

Lizzie made her way home mulling over what she had learnt. Something was bothering her but she was not sure exactly what it was. When she got home she kept herself busy watering and making sure the beans were climbing up their bamboo poles properly.

She dug up a few potatoes and washed them ready for tea. She also harvested some rhubarb and stewed it with root ginger and oranges to make a sorbet. The kitchen had a warm and inviting smell about it when she was cooking and this always made her feel happy and content.

The phone rang again. Lizzie realised she had not missed having a phone at all and it was becoming a bit of a nuisance.

'Hello?'

'Oh Lizzie, it's me again,' said Sally. 'I'm not really sure what to do. Fiona's been sent home from school with stomach pains again. I've given her some paracetamol and she's having a sleep, but I don't know if I ought to bother the doctor again or call Richard . . . '

'Well, see what she's like when she wakes up. Would you like me to call round? I could collect Sidney again for you, if it helps.'

'That's kind of you, but he's being dropped off today, as I took him and another little boy in this morning. I just . . . I'm sorry to bother you, I'm just not thinking straight at the moment.'

'Well, if there is anything I can do, just ask,' offered Lizzie.

'Thank you,' said Sally and for the first time Lizzie noticed a softening in Sally's voice. Lizzie cold tell she was close to tears. 'I'll give you a ring when she wakes up and let you know how she is.'

Lizzie wasn't surprised when, a few minutes later, the phone rang again. Sally's voice had an uncharacteristic tremble in it. 'I just wondered if, if you weren't too busy . . . '

'Do you need a hug?' offered Lizzie in her open, friendly way. She didn't wait for an answer. 'I'll be over in a few minutes.'

Fiona was just stirring as Lizzie arrived. 'I did bring a few peppermint leaves. You can infuse them and make peppermint tea which is supposed to be good for bad stomachs.'

'I'll give anything a try, although now she's woken up she seems fine again.'

'Does Richard know?' asked Lizzie.

'I did give him a ring. He was due to come back next Tuesday, but I think he was going to change a few things around and try and get home earlier.'

Just then the doorbell rang and Sally went to answer it. It was Sidney home from nursery with his friend.

'Fee!' called Sidney running into the lounge and seeing her lying on the sofa he dived on her to give her a big hug.

'Careful Sidney she's not feeling too well again.'

'Don't worry,' said Sidney. 'I'll mend her.' Sally looked at him and then at Lizzie.

Sidney took Fiona's arm and was pretending to bandage it up. His friend got hold of her leg and was copying Sidney.

'That tickles!' squealed Fiona and they all started laughing.

It was typical that then the real doctor pulled up with her medicine bag to see the patient who was too ill to come to surgery and needed a home visit.

'She was doubled over in pain earlier. I had to carry her from the school office to the car because she couldn't walk . . . ' Fiona was now chasing the two little boys around the lounge while the adults looked on.

'I'd just like to feel her stomach while

I'm here,' said the doctor.

Fiona did as she was told and lay back down on the sofa for the doctor to feel her tummy. She did still feel a bit tender but the real pain had gone.

The doctor was just packing away her stethoscope when Richard arrived.

'Daddy!' called Fiona who leapt up and gave him a hug. Sidney joined in.

'Not much wrong now,' said the doctor as she made her way out to her car and off to the next patient.

'Perhaps I was wrong,' said Sally quietly to Lizzie. 'Maybe she does miss him more than I realised.' Sally shook her head wearily. 'Maybe I do treat them differently, I don't mean to. I always try to be fair. I try to be a good mother but . . . '

A tear escaped, Sally roughly brushed it away. 'I'm sorry,' she said.

'You do a great job with them both and I know it isn't easy when you're on your own a lot. Is there any chance Richard could find a job closer to home?'

'It is something we've been talking about. He hates having to leave the children and he misses out on so many things — especially at this time of year when there's sports day and Fiona's in her school play and they've both got school trips to go on.'

Sally sniffed again and Lizzie put her arm round to comfort her. Richard walked into the kitchen and smiled at Lizzie. He had always been disappointed that the two women he loved most had never hit it off.

'Can I join in?' he said.

'Oh, Richard. I'm so sorry, I shouldn't have bothered you at work, she seems fine now, but honestly I was so worried about her. You wouldn't believe it to look at her now but she was in agony at school and I suppose I just panicked.'

'Well the important thing is that she is OK now,' said Richard giving his wife a hug.

Lizzie was invited, this time, to share the family meal and it was getting dark by the time she set off for home.

'Shall I walk you home?' asked Richard. Lizzie was confident about walking the short distance home but welcomed a little time alone with her brother. 'Thank you that would be nice.'

'It was good to see you and Sally getting on better,' he said when they had left the house. 'She's always been so envious of you.'

'Envious of me?' said Lizzie in astonishment. 'She's the one who's got a wonderful husband, two lovely children and a sought after home.'

'That's not the way she sees things. You had a career, you can cook, do those wonderful flower arrangements, grow anything and the children love you to bits.'

'But I'm not their mother and they love her even more.'

'I'm not sure that Sally always sees that. She is someone who likes everything to look right and, forgive me for saying this, I love her dearly, but sometimes I don't think she always gets her priorities right.'

'She's really worried about Fiona. What do you think is wrong with her?'

'I think it's probably a grumbling appendix and I dare say it will flare up again and we'll take her into hospital and they'll have to operate.'

'Well let's hope that's sooner rather than later.'

The following morning Lizzie was in her garden harvesting a few strawberries, raspberries and blueberries for her breakfast when she heard voices.

'Hello,' said Jack with a smile. 'I was hoping I'd see you again.' Lizzie smiled and realised she too had been hoping she would see him again. 'This is Joe. He's a builder and is going to give me a quote on next door.'

Lizzie and Joe politely shook hands. 'So you're moving in next door?' she asked, trying to hide her surprise.

'It won't be just yet as it needs a bit of work, but I'd like to as soon as I can.' He cleared his throat and asked, 'Would it be at all possible to have a look and see what you've done with your property?'

'No problem at all,' said Lizzie stepping back and opening the little gate for them to enter. 'It's not very grand, but it is home.' She said and opened the front door for them.

As it was basically a two up, two down cottage, the tour did not take long. Both men were very complimentary unlike the media men.

While Lizzie made them all a cup of tea, Joe disappeared next door to work on his quote.

'Where do the children sleep?' asked Jack and then he quickly added, 'I'm sorry, it's really none of my business.'

Lizzie put a mug of tea down in front of him at the wooden kitchen table. She smiled. 'You must mean Fiona and Sidney. They're my niece and nephew. They live in that new estate over there,' she pointed in the rough area of the old farm. 'They have slept over once or twice — usually they've had sleeping bags on the floor in my room. More often I stay over with them when I baby-sit. They have a guest room which I use.'

Jack now had a big grin on his face, but before he could explain, Joe walked up the garden path pulling a goat.

'Look what I found in your garden, Mr Curtis!'

Lizzie stood up quickly and lifted a metal chain with a leather lead from a hook on the kitchen wall.

'I'm so sorry,' she said and clipped the lead to the collar around Paddy's neck. 'You must think he's always getting out. He's been as good as gold for ages, but just recently he's been a bit of a Houdini!'

'Don't worry, I'm sure he hasn't done any damage. In fact, if he'll eat the grass you can leave him next door.'

'That's a bit of a myth. He will graze on grass, but only if there's nothing else. Sheep make better lawnmowers than goats.' Lizzie laughed.

'Should I invest in a couple of

sheep?' Jack asked as Lizzie led Paddy back out of the kitchen and in to the farmer's field.

When Lizzie returned a little while later, having picked a few early plums on her way, the two men were still sitting at her kitchen table discussing various interior designs.

'We could knock this old wash house down,' suggested Joe, 'Or make it into a utility room?'

'I'd much rather use it as my workroom. My lathe would fit in there.'

'Are you an engineer?' asked Lizzie as she leant over the plans. It was strange to see a mirror image of her own home.

'Yes, but my hobby has always been woodwork and that's what I intend to do here. Don't worry I won't make too much noise and maybe the wood-shavings could be used like chip bark or something for your garden . . . '

'I'd have to give you something in return,' said Lizzie, always quick to retain her independence.

'Do you have anything in mind?'

asked Jack looking at her with a smile as though he was noticing her for the first time. Lizzie could feel herself blushing and turned round to fetch the kettle and top up the mugs of tea.

'I'll happily trade you some apples when your mulberries are ripe.'

'Mulberries?' asked Jack.

'You've got a lovely old mulberry tree in your front garden. I have to admit now that I've picked them in the past as I didn't know who owned the cottage and they were just going to waste and I couldn't let that happen.'

'I don't think I've ever tasted mulberries,' said Jack, 'so I'm sure you can help yourself.'

'Here,' said Lizzie offering him a small jar of homemade mulberry jam. 'It's lovely on warm scones. They're not sweet, but my favourite is mulberry crumble.'

'Sounds delicious. I'm not much of a cook, can you make wine with them?'

'I'm not sure, but if you like making wine there's lot of elders around for making elderflower champagne or cordial and elderberry wine.'

Joe collected up all his papers and handed Lizzie his dirty cup.

'Thanks for the tea,' he turned to Jack. 'I'll get this all typed up and let you have the quote as soon as possible. I'll drop it in to the pub shall I?'

'Is it habitable next door?' asked Jack. Joe looked thoughtful.

'I wouldn't fancy it. There's no mod cons and only an outside loo, but the roof's good.'

'Well, maybe if I just camp out in the front room while you do the bathroom upstairs and then get to work on the kitchen. If I'm in your way, I can always move back to the pub.'

'It must be all the craze these days, living with just the bare basics. There was a piece in The Chronicle last night about someone living in the sticks with no TV or computer.'

Lizzie shivered at the thought of Paul pestering her again. Joe and Jack shook hands and Joe made his way back to his van.

'If you need any help moving in,' started Lizzie. 'I'm afraid I haven't got a van or anything, but I'm sure my brother would lend us his mower.'

'Thanks, that's very kind. You've made me feel very welcome already. I wonder if . . . ' Just at that moment Joe came running up the path again, but this time there was no goat in tow.

'Look!' he called and waved the newspaper at them. He opened it up to the middle pages and showed them a brief article on Lizzie and her sparse little home with a picture of Sidney shelling peas and lots more photos of her home. The black and white pictures made it look cold and drab.

'How dare he!' cried Lizzie. 'Just wait until I see him!' she seethed and both men decided it was time to go.

4

Once more Richard was home. This time he had taken some holidays and had promised to look seriously for a more local job. Sally had organised another special meal to welcome him back. This time she had invited Lizzie and a different circle of friends including a new neighbour.

'He's about your age, and quite nice looking,' said Sally to Lizzie the following week.

'You're not match-making are you?' asked Lizzie with a heavy heart.

'Of course not,' said Sally quickly, but not with conviction.

'I hope you weren't trying to fix me up with that awful man from the newspaper, too.'

'Paul? I thought he was quite nice. Certainly good-looking and with money, even if, well I have to admit, he wasn't really your type.'

'I can assure you we have absolutely nothing in common, except perhaps determination,' admitted Lizzie. She had visited him recently having seen the piece in the paper and had told him what she thought of him, but then, the very next day she was sure she'd seen his red Jaguar near her home.

Lizzie sat through another evening making polite small talk with friends of Sally's. The neighbour turned out, much to Lizzie's relief, to be very happily married and just getting the house ready for when his children finished their schooling elsewhere in the country and join him in their new home.

'Sorry,' said Sally at the end of the evening. 'I realise it can't have been much fun for you. Next time why don't you bring someone along? You must keep in touch with people you used to teach with.'

Lizzie was touched that in all the years she had known Sally, she felt this was the first time she had really seen things from her point of view as well as her own. Not only that, she had come up with a solution.

However, Lizzie was not sure that she really wanted to attend another of Sally's dinner parties. She knew her sister-in-law meant well. She knew she spent a lot of time with her children and did not enjoy cooking, but Lizzie couldn't help feeling it was such a waste of money buying expensive food from the farm shop. It tasted delicious, but Lizzie knew she could do better.

She was debating with herself whether she should offer to cook a meal for Sally and Richard and maybe even their friends, or whether she should actually offer to host her own dinner party.

A cry came from upstairs. Sally shot up the stairs taking two at a time. It was Fiona again. She looked pale and scared and was holding her tummy.

Richard wasted no time and called the out-of-hours service. Within a few minutes a doctor arrived. Fiona recoiled as he tried to feel her tender stomach.

The doctor noted the recent history she'd had of tummy aches and suggested they take her in to hospital again. The doctor phoned the hospital and told them to get a bed ready for her.

'Don't worry,' Lizzie told Richard. 'I'll sleep here with Sidney and take him back with me in the morning.'

Lizzie lay on the guest bed fully clothed. She had promised to stay with Sidney, but part of her wished he would wake up so she could take him home with her to Milkmaid's Cottage. For one thing she liked to be in her own bed and secondly she always did one last round at night just to check that all was well. She knew she had put the chickens away because she knew she was going to be late, but she had expected to be home.

Lizzie thought about Jack and wondered if he was staying next door in

Mulberry Cottage. It made no difference, she had no phone number for him, and she didn't even know if he had a phone.

She closed her eyes and tried to sleep and must have dozed for a while.

After a while she woke up again and this time she knew she'd been dreaming about Jack. She was going over the time when he and the builder, Joe, had been in her kitchen sipping tea. She was sure Joe had called him Mr Curtis. That name had rung a bell at the time, but even now she could not place where she'd heard it.

Lizzie got up and made herself a pot of tea. She wondered how they were getting on at the hospital and whether Fiona felt any better.

While she was waiting for the kettle to boil, Lizzie flicked through the telephone directory and found the number for the local pub. She looked at the time and thought it was too late to call, but made a note of the number so she could call in the morning to see if

Jack was still a resident.

The following morning Lizzie could hear Sidney getting up. She now felt really tired, partly because she'd been up a few hours in the night when she could not sleep and partly because she was worried about her niece.

Gently she explained to Sidney that Fiona had had another bad tummy ache and the doctor had been called.

'The doctor wasn't sure what was wrong with her so he suggested they take her into hospital for lots of doctors to have a look and to see if they can find out what is wrong'

'Me doctor,' said Sidney.

'Is that what you want to be when you grow up?'

He nodded.

'Breakfast,' said Sidney leading her to the kitchen.

'When you've finished your breakfast and cleaned your teeth, we'll go over to my house and check on the animals. We'll leave a note for your mummy and daddy so they'll know where you are.'

'Ginty,' said Sidney with a mouthful of cereal.

'Have you thought of being a vet rather than a doctor?' Lizzie asked her four-year-old nephew. 'You know, an animal doctor. I think you'd like that as you like animals so much.'

'Fiona's doctor first, then vet,' he told her as though it was easy to change from one professional role to another.

Lizzie was surprised to see a skip outside Mulberry Cottage and dust billowing from an upstairs window where the builders were beginning work on the bathroom.

Sidney was fascinated by a small rotavator that was churning up the front garden around the mulberry tree.

'Mind you don't damage the roots of the tree,' she yelled above the noise of the machine.

It looked as though Sidney could have spent all day just watching the workmen as they dug up the ground, filled the skip and appeared to be ripping the place apart. There was no sign of Jack.

Eventually Sidney agreed to come and collect the eggs and feed the goats. They were used to a routine and were now making lots of noise, as they were hungry for their breakfast and a bit of company.

The morning flew past. There were always jobs to do in the garden and every time Lizzie picked something there was another job to prepare it in the kitchen.

This morning they had picked a feast of strawberries, raspberries and blueberries that Lizzie kept in a small pot, as she liked these on her cereal in the morning.

They then stewed some more rhubarb for desserts. They ate plums from the tree and picked a variety of vegetables for tea or for freezing for the winter.

Lunch was a simple potato and cabbage soup followed by an apple from the tree. They had just finished when Richard strolled up the path looking tired. He hugged them both and they all sat in the garden to hear his news.

'I've just nipped out to get some food and a few bits and pieces. Fiona is stable again but they haven't actually done anything. Two doctors seem sure it's her appendix, but two others argue that it's a bit high up and they think it could be something else. They're not sure what. The poor thing has had so many tests this morning. They keep poking her and taking blood.'

'Are they letting her home?' asked Lizzie.

'They did mention it, but Sally has dug her heels in, she's refusing to take her home until they find out what it is. I think she was so cross because they didn't seem to believe her last time and just fobbed her off, now there's no denying that something is wrong, we just don't know what it is.'

'Oh well, she's in the best place.'

'She might be,' said Richard with

feeling. 'But it's the worst place ever for a parent. They provide the child with a meal three times a day but absolutely nothing for the parent. I can understand it's all extra cost, but we can't even buy anything.'

'I thought there was a café,' Lizzie said. 'I'm sure I've had a cup of tea when I've been in to visit.'

'There is a restaurant on the bottom floor, but we're on the top floor and Fiona just cries if we're out of her sight. She was asleep when I slipped out. I can't be long, as I've got some shopping to do. I'm going to buy a kettle and teabags and things for all the parents to use and some cup-a-soups, not to mention a decent meal for poor Sally, she's exhausted. I don't know how she'd manage if she was on her own.'

'Well I'll make sure I don't just look after Sidney but take her in some meals as well.'

'Sorry, I didn't mean to sound ungrateful. Thank you so much for looking after Sidney. I knew he'd be fine with you. Are you OK to keep him for a bit, until we know what's going on?'

'No problem. It's lovely to have his company.'

Richard turned to look at the cottage next door as a lorry beeped its way up the lane to collect the full skip and deliver a new empty one.

'I didn't know it was lived in,' he said.

'It wasn't. I'm still not really sure who owns it. Mrs Marshall up at the farm said there was some story attached to it.'

'Yes,' said Richard, but rather than tell the story he rose to go. 'I don't want to be too long, Fiona's a bit scared and very clingy at the moment.'

'Can we come and visit her?'

'Maybe tomorrow would be best. In fact, if you did come tomorrow afternoon and stayed with her maybe it could give Sally and I a break. I'm sure Sally would love to come home for a bath or a nap and I can take her out for a decent meal instead of making do on simple snacks.'

'We'll see you tomorrow afternoon then,' said Lizzie and Sidney waved.

'I'll give you a call if they do eventually take her down to the operating theatre.'

The following day there had been no call from Richard, so Lizzie assumed there was not really any news. She and Sidney had been out for a walk, but took the phone with them.

On returning from their walk Lizzie's heart sank as she saw the distinctive red Jaguar outside the cottages. She took Sidney's hand and led him a different way home where there were some damsons that were ripe and always fell to the ground to be eaten by animals or left to go to waste.

'These will be nice for pudding,' said Lizzie as she collected them up. Sidney made a face. 'Don't worry we'll give them a good wash first.'

The route back to the house via the damsons took them round the back of the cottages. As they approached Lizzie was sure she could hear raised voices. The closer they got the more clear it was that there was an argument going on and it was coming from Mulberry Cottage.

Lizzie slowed right down as she did not want to intrude on the argument and didn't want Sidney to witness any unpleasant scene.

The voices rose and the shouting went on for some time before Paul, the editor, slammed the front door and stormed off down the path of Mulberry Cottage. Lizzie could now see his car parked near the skip. She was sure that earlier it had been parked outside her own house.

Lizzie was very keen to know what had been going on with Paul and her neighbour or his builders. She was also keen to know either from Mrs Marshall or from her brother about the story linked with the house next door, but most of all, as she opened her own front door, she wondered how Fiona was and what news there was from the hospital.

Sidney knew his mum's mobile number and tried to phone it but it was switched off. 'Don't worry. I'm sure Daddy will pop round and see us when he can. Let's hope she's OK and we can go and visit her tomorrow. Would you like to draw her a nice picture?'

He sat in the back garden lying on the grass drawing Henny Penny, one of the bantams. It was easy to collect up their feathers, which he carefully stuck on to the picture.

Lizzie milked McGinty and watered the tomatoes and cape gooseberries. She picked the ripe tomatoes and started to think what she would cook them with for tea.

Out of the corner of her eye she noticed Joe the builder packing up for the day along with another young lad.

'How's it going?' she asked.

'We've made a good start,' said Joe. 'The boss is in if you want to have a look for yourself.'

Lizzie thought back to Paul leaving a

little while ago in such a rage. Joe and his young lad had obviously been in the house and it seems, so too had Jack. She wondered what was going on now.

'Hello!' said Jack, popping his head out of the front room window. 'How's Fiona?'

'Still in hospital, no news really. Sidney and I are hoping to go and visit her tomorrow afternoon. It'll give my brother and sister-in-law a bit of a break too. Thank you for asking after her. We'll fill you in when we get back tomorrow.'

'Are you staying here tonight?' asked Jack. Lizzie looked at Sidney.

'What shall we do, Sid, shall we sleep here or do you want your own bed?'

Before he could answer, Jack said, 'I was thinking of having a bonfire and wondered if you'd like to join me. That's if you haven't got any washing out or anything.'

'Fire!' said Sydney making his decision.

'I've got some nice big baking

potatoes, shall I start them off in the oven for tea?' Lizzie asked Jack.

'Sounds good.' He then turned to Sidney. 'Are you any good at climbing trees?' Sidney nodded. 'Would you help me pick some apples? They're nice eaters. I had one earlier.'

While Lizzie did her daily spot of weeding, Sidney happily climbed up the apple tree and threw apples down to Jack. Together they then went round the garden picking up twigs and sticks to make a fire.

'Come on Jack, let's play catch!' called Sidney. Lizzie's jaw dropped, not only had her nephew come out with a full sentence but he was confidently playing ball with a man he hardly knew. He was usually so quiet and shy and even more so at the moment with Fiona in hospital and his mum and dad away with her.

The mobile phone rang and Lizzie was glad to hear Sally's voice even though she sounded tired and anxious.

'Fiona's gone for a scan. There's a long wait, so I've just nipped out for a bit of fresh air in the hospital car park where I can use the phone. They're still doing tests, they now think there's something wrong with her gut rather than appendix. I suppose it's good that they are thorough, but these tests seem to be taking forever and she's been sick and I can't sleep in the hospital.'

'They provide a camp bed but no bedding, you're meant to bring in your own sleeping bag and pillow. I don't go camping so I haven't got one, so I rolled up my sweatshirt and used my coat as a blanket, but it was cold with all the windows open and there's beeps going off from the monitors and children crying and then at about six they get everyone up. How's Sidney?'

Lizzie looked out of her front door and watched as Sidney and Jack chased butterflies around the garden and then feel into a heap laughing like two happy children.

'He's fine. In fact I think he's made a new friend,' said Lizzie with a smile.

5

Lizzie hid a yawn as the embers of the fire began to die away. She shivered despite having put on a jumper and having the warm body of Sidney, now sound asleep, curled up in a rug on her lap.

'You're getting cold. Do you want me to put on some more logs, I'm sure I could get it to light again.'

'I ought to take this little man up to bed,' said Lizzie. 'Thank you for a lovely evening. A friend I used to teach with once remarked that I spend hours upon hours in the garden, but rarely sit back and just enjoy it. She was right.'

'Well in that case we'll have to do it again. I think Sidney enjoyed it too.' They both laughed as they recalled him offering to stand up and entertain them with his song. It was a nursery rhyme that they weren't familiar with and it didn't make sense, but he sang it beautifully.

'Thank you for that too,' said Lizzie seriously. 'Sidney has always been shy and quiet, but he's really come out of his shell these last few days. You bring out the best in him.'

'Are you sure it's not you that brings out the best in him?' said Jack, equally seriously. He offered a hand to help take the sleeping child out of her lap so she could get out of the makeshift seat.

As he cradled the sleeping Sidney in his arms, Lizzie tucked the rug around him and they turned to take him inside. They were disturbed by the sound of youths coming noisily up the path. They didn't seem to be doing any harm. They were just laughing and talking loudly. It seemed all the more intrusive because of the still summer's evening.

'Nice apples!' called one lad as they approached the cottages.

'Let's get him inside,' suggested Jack.

'Nice place to go scrumping!' said another voice.

'There's a sleeping bag on my bed, would you put him in there, and I'll be up in a minute.'

'Don't you want the bed?'

'I'll be fine in the chair. I didn't sleep much the other night and now it's really caught up with me. I could sleep anywhere,' admitted Lizzie as she hooked a strand of loose hair round her ear.

'Good. I noticed you yawning. I'm glad you weren't bored with my company!' He smiled a generous smile — his whole face came alive from the laugh lines around his eyes, the curve of his cheeks and the twinkle in his eye. 'Would you rather take him up yourself so I can put out the fire?' offered Jack, glancing at the rabble of boys approaching her cottage.

'I'll be fine. Off you go, he must be heavy.'

Jack glanced round at the youths who were very close now. 'I'll be down in a minute,' he said reassuringly.

Lizzie had always prided herself on

being independent and yet now, for the first time she could ever remember, she felt comforted by the fact that she wasn't alone and, dare she say it, that she felt Jack cared what happened to her. She quickly brushed the feelings aside.

Lizzie went back through the gate in the fence between their two gardens and collected up their things. It had turned out to be quite a feast around the fire.

She put Jack's things in his one barely liveable room and then returned to the garden. The fire was almost completely out now but the light from her bedroom lit up the garden enough for her to see.

Lizzie stamped on the remains of the fire to make sure it was safely out. She gathered her belongings and then looked up as one of the lads jumped over her fence and into her garden.

'Brian Potter! What would your mum say?' she said in her teacher's voice. There was stunned silence for a moment. The boy froze in mid stride as he headed for her apple tree.

'Miss Elliot? I heard you moved to the country,' said one of the lads. Brian held his head low and carefully opened the picket gate to let himself out.

'Sorry, Miss,' he mumbled.

'How's your brother now? Last time I saw him he'd got his leg in plaster.'

'All mended now Miss, but Lee broke his arm playing football last week.' The group pushed Lee to the front to show off his plastered arm.

'I scored the best goal though, Miss, you should have seen it, a right cracker it was and we won the game!'

'Was it very painful?' asked Lizzie.

'Not that bad, Miss, but we had to wait ages in casualty. That were the worst bit.'

They caught up on old news for another few minutes before Jack joined them to see what was going on.

'I didn't know you'd got married, Miss?' said Lee. 'Remember when you caught us picking roses from the back of the school?'

'I remember,' said Lizzie. 'There was a pretty rose garden at the back of the Headmaster's office. I'd never have caught you, but you left a trail of rose petals!'

'You promised us that the only time we could throw rose petals was at your wedding!'

'I'll have to remember that,' said Jack and everyone looked at him.

A cry came from upstairs as Sidney stirred. 'Sorry lads, must go!' called Lizzie as she ran up the stairs leaving Jack to see the boys off. When she returned the boys had gone and Jack was in his own home. Where her home had suddenly seemed alive and vibrant, it now seemed more than empty. It seemed desolate.

Lizzie realised how important it was in her life to be surrounded by people. Reluctantly she realised she missed teaching and having a class who became like her family. What she didn't miss was the endless list of things to do.

The following day, Lizzie took Sidney to see Fiona in hospital. Fiona looked a bit pale and was bored. They had watched lots of DVDs, read lots of stories and done every jigsaw puzzle over 50 pieces.

Sally looked equally as pale and very tired. Lizzie gave her a hug and Sally almost crumpled in her arms. Lizzie was taken by surprise. Sally was always so strong and capable.

'Look, I plan to be here all afternoon. If you like, and if Fiona is happy, why don't you go home for a few hours? I bet you could do with a nap, or at least a change of view.'

In response Sally squeezed Lizzie's hand. Again Lizzie was surprised. Sally had always been aloof and rather distant with Lizzie. It was, Lizzie always felt, that Sally was somehow superior because she was a mum and Lizzie had never been lucky enough.

'I'd be grateful,' Sally was saying. 'Let's just check with Fiona. I'm sure

Richard told you, she's been really clingy lately, although she does seem a bit brighter today.'

As they approached Fiona's hospital bed, Fiona was in full flow showing and telling poor little Sidney what she'd already been through.

'And then they put another needle in here to give me a drip. I think it's some sort of medicine to take the pain away.' Fiona looked up. 'Hello, Auntie Liz,' she said and leant forward to give Lizzie a hug.

'And how are you feeling today?' asked Lizzie.

'A bit better, but we're waiting to go up to another, even bigger hospital in London.'

'Fiona love, Auntie Liz and Sidney are going to spend the afternoon with you. Would you mind if I nip home for a little while? I can bring you in a clean nightdress and bring in some more books to read,' asked Sally.

Fiona considered this for a few minutes. Lizzie was in a position to stand back and watch how these three people whom she loved so dearly were all changing and developing almost before her eyes.

Fiona had always been bouncy and confident. They'd joked how she was 8 going on 18!

Sally had changed from being super-efficient but a little cold and aloof, to being loving and full of hugs as if she had, at last, seen what was really important in her life and that was her children rather than the state of her house or how her hair looked.

Sidney too had altered. A boy of very few words most of the time, was growing in confidence.

'Lizzie?' a voice broke into her thoughts. It was Richard, he'd been to talk to the nurse in charge to get an update.

'Sorry, I was miles away.'

'Is Daddy going home too?' asked Fiona.

'Would you mind?' asked Lizzie. 'Sidney and I have loads of things to tell you, and we've bought you some different things to do.'

'You will come back?' asked Fiona.

'Of course we will, love. Is there anything else you can think of that you need from home?' Fiona shook her head, kissed her parents goodbye and waved until they were out of sight.

'Jack and I made a huge fire,' said Sidney. 'And we had tea round the fire and sang songs.'

Lizzie could see that Fiona was aware that something was different, but it was as if she could not quite put her finger on what it was.

'And then this morning I collected three eggs and we had them for breakfast.'

'Who is Jack?' asked Fiona. 'Does he go to nursery with you?' she asked and both Sidney and Lizzie laughed.

'Jack's the man who lives next door,' explained Lizzie. Fiona looked puzzled.

'I didn't think anyone lived next door. I thought it was falling down.'

'It does need a lot of work on it. I

think Jack is just staying in one room. He's sort of camping. He's not really moved in. I don't think he can be very comfortable.'

The three of them sat on the hospital bed chatting for about an hour and then Fiona and Sidney did a puzzle together. Lizzie went to see if she could get them a drink.

Lizzie returned to the children and watched them finish the puzzle together.

'Are you able to walk?' Lizzie asked.

'Of course I can walk!' said Fiona. 'But I do need to take my drip with me. I couldn't walk the other day,' she confided in them. 'Mummy had to wheel me about in a wheelchair. I was in so much pain I was all bent over.'

'Is it much better now?' asked Lizzie.

'Are you coming home soon?' asked Sidney. 'You can come and sleep at Auntie Lizzie's.'

'I think I have to go to this other hospital first. They don't really know what's wrong with me and so I have to have more tests.'

Lizzie tried to change the subject. She asked if anyone from school had been in to visit her and Fiona said that her best friend had and maybe someone else was going to come at the weekend.

'The Year Sixes did a Talent Show which was really good and I missed it. Laura did say someone filmed it and maybe I could borrow it and watch it some time, but it's not the same as being there.'

Lizzie caught the attention of one of the nurses and asked if it were possible to take Fiona, in a wheelchair, with her drip, to the café for a drink and a change of scenery.

'I'll just go and check,' said the nurse and some time later she returned and told them it would be fine as Fiona was just waiting to be transferred to another hospital.

'Come on then,' said Lizzie, 'This will be quite an adventure, I've never pushed a wheelchair before!'

It was a slow journey down to the basement café. Sidney pushed Fiona for part of the way, while Lizzie steadied the drip which was like a pole on wheels.

Fiona was exhausted by the time they returned to the ward and she fell asleep. Sidney was amused by the children's programmes on the TV as he hadn't seen any television for the last few days since he'd been staying with Lizzie.

Lizzie wandered up and down the children's ward and realised that there was nowhere for a parent to boil a kettle and drink a hot drink safely away from the children.

Fiona's tea arrived just as she was stirring, and soon after, Richard and Sally returned looking more refreshed.

It seemed Richard had to go abroad again to sort out some problem. He had already put it off twice, so this time he really had to go. However, Sidney was more than happy to stay with his aunt. In fact when he was asked what he'd like for his forthcoming birthday, he asked for a chicken of his own.

When Lizzie and Sidney arrived back

at Milkmaid's Cottage, they saw a strange sight. The house was full of workmen again. The new skip was full but under the front room window the grass was moving about in a wild fashion.

They crept through the broken fence between the two properties, in now what had become a makeshift gate. Sydney stalked the grass like a tiger only to find Jack, on his hands and knees, trying to clear a patch of ground.

'This is going to take forever!' he said. He stood and wiped his muddy hands down his trousers. His hands and knees were dripping with mud. 'How's Fiona?'

'Bored. They're still not quite sure what's wrong, so they're waiting for a free bed at The Chelsea and Westminster Hospital in London.'

'And your sister?'

'My sister-in-law is finding it hard, but I think she's learnt a lot from the experience and will be a better person for it, in the end.'

'Well, my back aches and I've very little to show for all my efforts. I discovered I've got a lovely plum tree at the back, so I picked some, would you like to join me? I must go and have a wash first. That part of the garden must have been a pond at one time. It's really boggy.'

They shared the plums. 'When my pears are ready you'll have to help me pick them Sidney. And then we can share those too. Shall I make a cup of tea?' offered Lizzie. 'I'm going to make Sidney some dinner anyway.'

'Can we have a fire again?' he asked excitedly.

'Well, I did happen to buy some marshmallows when I was in town earlier and I believe they cook well on a fire.' Lizzie and Sidney laughed as Jack held up the packet and shook them temptingly.

'Sidney, if I let you have some marshmallows, after you've eaten your tea, do you think your daddy would let me borrow his lawnmower?'

'Daddy's away,' explained Sidney.

'I'll speak to Richard as soon as he gets home. He has some problem to sort out, but I know he'll be back as soon as he can.'

The next few days were busy and eventful. Fiona was transferred to The Chelsea and Westminster Hospital awaiting a biopsy to aid the staff in providing a diagnosis.

Jack had most of his land rotovated, but kept a small lawn at the front around the mulberry tree so that the roots were not damaged and he had somewhere to sit and enjoy the evening sun.

Lizzie called in at the farm and chatted with Mrs Marshall while Sidney was at nursery. 'Tell me again about Mulberry Cottage, last time we talked about it, you said there was some story about it.'

'A sad tale yes,' began Mrs Marshall with her arms folded yet again. 'I can't remember the details, but it must have been twenty, twenty-five years ago. We sold the cottage to this lovely young couple who were getting married. She was local, I think, but he wasn't. They didn't have much money so they were going to gradually do up the cottage after they'd married. Then, very close to the wedding day — I'm not sure if it was even the day or two before, she was killed in a car crash.'

'The wedding then became a funeral and no one ever moved into Mulberry Cottage.'

'That's dreadful. It must have happened while I was away at teacher training college otherwise I'm sure I'd remember that, especially if she was local. You don't remember her name?'

Mrs Marshall shook her head and served a customer at the farm shop. Lizzie bought a few things and was about to leave.

'It just got worse after that,' continued Mrs Marshall.

'Pardon?'

'The brother of the bride, or maybe the groom, decided he'd buy the cottage and do it up. It's a pretty place after all. But then no sooner had he got married, she realised she'd made a big mistake and went off with her childhood sweetheart. It was so sad. I'm sure she never meant to hurt him, but she'd married on the rebound and realised she'd married the wrong one.'

'Couldn't she have tried to make a go of it?' asked Lizzie.

'I suppose she could. I remember thinking that myself, at the time, but looking back, I suppose she felt less damage would be done if she went straight away.'

'That must have been before I bought the cottage,' said Lizzie almost to herself.

'Oh yes, it must have been fifteen years ago, maybe more. Again, the chap didn't want to live there on his own and it just stayed empty.'

'But now I have a new neighbour,' said Lizzie anxious to drop his name into the conversation. 'His name's Jack and he seems very pleasant. He's great with Sidney, my nephew.'

Lizzie took her shopping and walked home mulling on their conversation. She realised she knew very little about Jack. She wondered if he knew of the history of the house and whether it was wise to tell him.

The phone was ringing when Lizzie opened her door. It was Sally. 'The doctor now thinks Fiona's got colitis. It's ulcers in her gut and is very painful. They've put her on steroids to control it and we hope to be home by the weekend. I can't wait to get back to normal.'

'Well thankfully Fiona's OK and it's nothing life threatening.'

'That's true. It's been an awful time and you won't believe how much the hospital said they thought it would cost to put in a kitchen and lounge for parents to use!' Sally told her a figure and the line crackled.

'I'd better go and fetch Sidney from nursery. It's his sports day this afternoon. Do you mind if I borrow your camera?'

'Of course not, wish him luck from

me. I'll try and call again to speak to him but it's difficult as we're not allowed phones on inside the hospital, I've just nipped out as Fiona was sleeping. I'd better get back to her.'

6

Sidney skipped back from sports day with his medals hanging around his neck.

Lizzie's phone rang. She could not get used to being outside, more or less miles from anywhere, at the bottom of the narrow track that led to her cottage, and to hear a phone ring.

'Hello, Liz. It's Sally. Just to let you know Fiona's eaten her first proper meal in ages! Is Sidney there?' Lizzie passed the phone over to Sidney and watched how naturally he assumed the pose of chatting on a mobile while walking back to Milkmaid's Cottage. The divide between past and present was getting hazy.

As Lizzie put the phone away and reached in her bag for her key, she noticed the red Jaguar that could only belong to Paul, the newspaperman, who

99

was beginning to stalk her, she felt.

'A little bird told me you lied. You do have a phone, admittedly not a land line, just a mobile but I thought you said . . . '

'When I spoke to you, I didn't have a phone but since then my sister-in-law bought me one, and even I have to admit that lately when my niece has been seriously ill, it has been useful.'

'I'm here to make you an offer you can't refuse!' he said smugly and Lizzie cringed. This man would not take no for an answer!

'Spit it out then,' said Lizzie. 'I need to get home and feed this hungry sportsman. He's won three medals you know.'

'So I can see.' Paul reached for his phone and seemed to just press a button or two and then spoke to someone on the phone, ignoring them, 'Got a photographer free?' he asked, and then to Lizzie he said, 'Which school?'

'Chestnut Nursery and Kindergarten,' said Lizzie.

'Is he going to take my picture for the paper?' asked Sidney excitedly.

'How would you feel if he did?' asked Lizzie marvelling at the way he had come out of his shell.

'I can show Mummy when she gets home,' he said simply.

Paul finished his curt conversation and turned again to Lizzie. 'My Advertising Manager is confident he can sell loads of advertising around a weekly feature on being green and looking after the environment and that sort of thing. It's fashionable at the moment, so name your price.'

Lizzie was about to repeat that she was not interested in his offer now or at all in the future but an inkling of an idea was stirring within her.

'You'd want me to write a short piece . . . '

'About 1000 words with photos — a sort of diary.'

'Daily? Weekly? Monthly?' Asked Lizzie.'

'We're a weekly paper. It would be

good to see how you cope in all the seasons — how low and miserable you are when we're all snug and warm at Christmas time, you know, the sort of thing.'

'I'll warn you now, even if times do get hard, I'm a positive sort of person, so it won't be all doom and gloom.'

'That's OK, my readers can read between the lines. Name your price, so I can double it for my advertising manager to hit his target — don't tell him that of course,' laughed Paul in a slimy sort of way. Lizzie nearly pulled out of the deal. She really did not feel happy doing business with a man she detested but . . .

'I need £50,000,' she said. 'It's not for me but it's needed for the hospital to build or refurbish a room to set aside for parents of sick children to use when the children are in hospital.'

Paul grinned. 'A sick child in the story, this gets better every minute. I can see a donation line . . . '

'Obviously my sister-in-law and I will

have to speak to the Trustees of the hospital first and you and I will need to lay down the rules.'

'Shall we set a meeting for this time next week, in my office followed by a press conference and launch of the,' he paused, 'Help the hospital campaign? Help the children? Got it! Green Goddess helps local hospital!'

'Mr . . . I'm sorry I don't think we were ever properly introduced.'

'Curtis, Paul Curtis,' he said and was about to shake her hand. 'No, we'll shake on the deal. I'll see you next week.' With that he was off in his red Jaguar.

Friday was like a big family reunion. Sally thankfully brought Fiona back from the London hospital, Richard flew home and had booked a fortnight's leave and Lizzie walked Sidney and his sleeping bag home along the rough path which was becoming churned up from the lorries visiting Mulberry Cottage.

Fiona had a bit of colour back in her

face and ate a huge meal followed by two puddings.

'The doctor warned me that the steroids would make her put on weight, but thinking about it, she had got really thin, so I suppose a little bit won't hurt.'

Sidney, despite having loved his adventures with Auntie Liz was pleased to be back in his own bed and made no fuss about going upstairs at bedtime. Fiona still lacked energy and was asleep before her brother.

'Now I've got the two of you together,' said Lizzie, 'there's something I want to discuss.'

Sally smiled, 'Anything to do with Uncle Jack?'

'Uncle Jack?' asked Richard. 'Who's he?'

'Sidney won't stop talking about making a huge fire with Uncle Jack and then helping Uncle Jack to find long sticks to toast marshmallows and then making a camp in the garden with guess who? Uncle Jack.'

'Jack's my neighbour,' said Lizzie shortly but she could feel herself blushing. 'It's got nothing to do with him actually.'

Sally put down a tray of little cups on the table and poured out coffee while Lizzie began to explain her idea.

'You're writing for the local paper and instead of paying you they will donate a sum of money to help the hospital provide a parents' room?'

'More or less,' said Lizzie. 'Sally, I know you must be really busy, but I wonder if you could come with me to the hospital in the next few days and discuss this with the Trustees, obviously we need to have their backing.'

'I'd be delighted. Actually it will do me the world of good to get my teeth into something, I've had so much time sitting and thinking.'

'Oh, and by the way, Richard, I was wondering if Jack could borrow your mower, he's trying to tame his garden. We've done quite a bit so far, but there's a patch of grass we're going to keep near the Mulberry.'

'We?' asked Sally.

'Of course you can borrow my mower,' said Richard. 'Do I get to meet and vet this young man?'

'He's not so much of a young man and it's not like that! He's just a neighbour, but he's been great with Sidney.'

The hospital trustees were delighted with the proposed launch of the fund to convert an old medical store into a parents' room. They were happy with the publicity from the local paper as this would only benefit their cause.

'We're a good team!' said Lizzie to Sally as they left the hospital feeling excited about this new project.

'I wasn't sure about that storage room when they first showed it to us. It was so dark and dismal. I imagine somewhere bright and airy, perhaps with a little courtyard garden, but that room didn't even have a window!'

'I know what you mean, but Jack's agreed to ask Joe, his builder, to come and give us a quote. Maybe they could knock through the outside wall and either put in a large window or patio doors. It does open into an enclosed area — anyway Joe will come up with some ideas and quotes and in the meantime we can raise the money to pay for it.'

'Thanks for this,' said Sally giving Lizzie a hug.

'Sally?' asked Lizzie, 'Would you come with me to the meeting with Paul? You know him better than I do and I can't say I like the man. I feel I need someone there on my side, sort of an independent witness.'

'I'm sure he can't be that bad, but I'm sure I'll be able to come as Richard's off and is enjoying being with the kids.'

Paul's office was as large as Lizzie's front room, but whereas her room was sparsely decorated with simple wooden furniture, his office was richly carpeted with a thick burgundy carpet. He had an enormous desk with a chair behind which was more like a throne. In front of it were two slightly smaller chairs and then to the left were two, two-seater settees, also in burgundy, around a coffee table.

'Good, so the hospital is in agreement. I had a call earlier. Have you brought Fiona with you?' Lizzie was surprised he remembered her name, but then saw a sketch from the newspaper's artists' studio launching the *Fiona Fund*.

'My daughter's on steroids at the moment and she doesn't quite look like herself. I don't think she'd want her photo taken just at the moment,' said Sally.

A woman, probably Paul's secretary, brought in a tray of tea and a file of papers.

'This is the agreement,' he said. 'Why don't yousit down there with a cup of tea and read through it, when you're ready you can sign it and off we go!'

Sally and Lizzie read through the document. 'This says I'll be writing weekly for a year!' said Lizzie. 'Did we agree a whole year?'

'Don't you remember I mentioned people would want to see the change of seasons? How you struggle in winter, how you feel spring in the air etc. etc.'

'All right, that's fine,' agreed Lizzie knowing that it would be quite a challenge but not impossible.

'Are you sure,' cautioned Sally. 'What about this bit about not being able to spend any money unless you've earned it? That's a bit hard.'

'If you're self sufficient I don't want you nipping down the supermarket for toilet rolls or to hire a DVD,' he laughed, 'Sorry that wouldn't be any use of you, you haven't got a TV or a DVD player!'

'What about paying bills like electricity etc.'?

'That's a direct debit, same as your gas supplier, they'll stay the same but think of your bank account as being frozen. From now on, everyday things you'll have to earn and you'll need to keep strict account of everything.'

'So I could ask Lizzie to baby-sit for me and either pay her in cash or pay her in toothpaste and deodorant?' asked Sally.

'Well, you're family, wouldn't she baby-sit for free?' asked the hard editor.

'She'll be too busy to baby-sit unless I can make it worth her while,' said Sally driving a hard bargain.

'OK, but the general rule is, family can help, not give you things, but cut your grass or give you a lift, but any one else can only help you in return for goods or services. It can be cash or you can barter if you have a glut of something. Understand?'

Eventually all the finer details were ironed out and Lizzie signed on the dotted line, conscious that the whole area would be concentrating on her life for the next year. This was a far cry from retiring to the countryside to be a bit of a recluse.

'So you finally accepted the bet?' asked

Jack when Lizzie eventually got home.

'How do you know?' asked Lizzie already wondering if she had done the right thing.

'It was on the local radio. You're quite a celebrity already!'

'Oh well, I don't stand around chatting, I've got work to do!' said Lizzie marching up her path and into the cold stone cottage. This was actually going to be harder than she thought.

The next few days were sunny and Lizzie took advantage of the good weather. She went mushrooming early in the morning and then spent the whole afternoon picking blackberries. In years gone by she would pick enough for a few pies to take to Sally's for Sunday lunch. This year she picked as many as she could find, to put in her freezer, just in case.

Lizzie was careful to note all that she did partly to give evidence to Paul, should he query anything, and partly so she could use it when she came to sit down and write her first diary entry.

The first night after she'd accepted the wager she found she could not sleep. Her idyllic life had been introduced to stress. Now she had to fend for herself. She was on her own.

The following day she was tired from a disturbed night. She wanted to phone Paul and check what would happen if she didn't make it, but now every resource became precious because she didn't know how she would replace it.

Sally had insisted on generously topping up the mobile phone credit. She reiterated that it was purely selfish as Lizzie might be needed in an emergency but Lizzie knew it was also Sally's way of helping.

'Fancy a cuppa?' called Jack from his side of the garden.

'Sorry, I've got to get these spring cabbages in and dig over that bed for winter spinach.'

'Maybe later?' suggested Jack.

'Yes, maybe later.' She agreed but later she was out gathering sticks for the fire and picking more blackberries to go with her autumn raspberries for tea.

Lizzie couldn't help noticing some of the things Jack was throwing away into the skip. She was horrified to notice a pile of chemicals. She left what she was doing and stormed over to Jack's side of the fence.

'I'm organic!' she announced. 'You're not gong to start spraying weed-killer all over the place are you?'

'This is my land,' Jack reminded her. 'I can spray weed-killer and insecticide wherever I want!'

'But I've been organic for years and your land has been fallow for years, don't go and spoil everything by spraying. There are lots of other ways of getting rid of things like blackfly.'

'I'm sure there are,' said Jack. 'You could have had that cup of tea after all, instead of just accusing me of being un-organic!'

Lizzie felt she didn't want to drink tea with the enemy and stormed off back to her side of the garden.

'In you go,' said Lizzie pushing

Paddy into the pen that evening. McGinty snuggled up to her waiting for a bit of attention. There was nothing she liked more than having her forehead and chin tickled. 'I haven't got time for that now,' snapped Lizzie. 'I've got the last of the rhubarb to cook tonight and potato soup to make and freeze and I need to start thinking what I can make for my family for Christmas . . . '

'Good job they don't answer back,' said a familiar mellow voice from nearby.

'I was talking to the goat, not to you!' snapped Lizzie. She could feel her shoulders tense and her neck was stiff. 'I'm sorry, I didn't mean to snap. I'm just tired.'

'I'll say goodnight,' said Jack. 'I just wanted to reassure you that I've every intention of gardening organically. You just never gave me a chance to say!' Lizzie felt so embarrassed she didn't even turn around.

The following day it was definitely

cooler and Lizzie picked the last of her tomatoes. She made tomato soup and froze what was left. It had been a good crop and she noted she would grow the same one again next year.

She was pleased when she looked in her little shed. She had reused a sack that had had goat mix in it, for storing her potatoes and another one had apples. She had trays of onions, shallots and garlic. All of these things should see her through the winter.

Lizzie went inside ready to prepare a marrow for her tea. Out of the window she saw the distinctive red Jaguar. Surely he hasn't come for the first instalment yet? She had planned to sit down and write it tomorrow.

She waited for the knock, but it didn't come. After a while, Lizzie became suspicious. She wondered if Paul was snooping round, checking up on her. She went to the front room and looked out of the window to try to see what he was up to.

There he was, as bold as brass,

talking with Jack. She could see Paul's face, he looked smug. Jack had his back to her. Again, she was reminded how similar they looked although very different in character. It then struck her.

Curtis! They were both called Curtis! They must be related. As she thought it, she felt physically ill, as though she'd been punched in the stomach. 'I bet Jack is only living in that one tiny room so he can spy on me for Paul!'

Lizzie, still armed with her marrow, marched outside and down her path to where the two men were talking.

'Mr Curtis,' she paused as they both looked at her. 'Paul, you didn't make it clear what would happen if I didn't make the whole year.'

'Giving up already?' he laughed.

'Give her a chance,' said Jack. 'She's been working really hard. She's up really early collecting mushrooms and then works all day and her light was on until gone midnight.'

'Are you spying on me?' Lizzie

accused him, 'I bet it was you who told Paul I had a phone.'

'Were you trying to conceal it?' asked Paul quickly.

'No, of course not but . . . ' she knew she'd fallen into his trap. 'So, if I don't actually make it self sufficient for a whole year, what happens?'

'Well obviously I don't pay up. That means the hospital doesn't get its money and the parents of those poor sick children don't get their relaxation room, and the wonderful, generous Green goddess will be . . . garbage?'

'Oh. I don't have to pay the money instead?'

'No, I'll waiver that bit for just one kiss!' he said. His watch or phone or something bleeped and he said, 'Must be off!' He blew her a kiss and strode off to his car. 'I'm expecting 'Week One' tomorrow, don't let me down.'

The following day Sally called round with the children. Fiona was chubbier than ever and obviously not happy about it.

'We're walking or cycling everywhere at the moment to keep fit while I'm on these tablets!' announced Fiona.

'I've brought you a few things,' said Sally. 'Shall I just leave them in the kitchen?'

'Thank you but you're not supposed to do that,' reminded Lizzie.

'If I were visiting a friend I might well take them a bunch of flowers — you grow your own, so I thought you might prefer a lovely crusty loaf of bread and some citrus fruit!'

'Sally you're an angel! I was only thinking how much I fancied an orange and whether I could try and grow oranges in my lounge.'

'Not this year I think, but I'm sure you'll save the pips and have a go.'

They stayed for a little while, but Sally wanted to make a move early because they could see a storm brewing.

'If you've written your first piece, I can take it and drop it into the newspaper office for you, we've got to go in to the chemist anyway.'

'Will you read it through first? It was much harder than I thought. I just had a list of things I'd done, but it didn't read very well, then I tried explaining things and it was too long so then I ended up just doing an introduction saying how long I'd lived here, what animals I've got and what I'm growing at the moment.'

'That sounds fine,' said Sally reading it rough.

'What's this?' asked Fiona. Lizzie laughed.

'I've been having a go at a few new skills. Your mum and dad gave me the spinning wheel years ago and I've been collecting up some goat hair. It's not going very well. I need Angora goats really as they have long hair and mine are Pygmy goats.'

'Pigs?' asked Sidney.

'Pygmies just mean small,' explained Lizzie, 'And yesterday I collected some willow which I'm soaking in order to try and do some basket weaving.'

'Come on,' called Sally. 'That article is fine, shame you're so tired. You don't really sound as though you are enjoying it.'

'It's too much like hard work at the moment and I can't really see it getting any better.'

'Chin up!' said Sally. 'Now we must go before it rains.'

The rains did come about half an hour later, along with thunder and lightning. Lizzie prayed that there wouldn't be any real damage or leaks.

As it eased off she checked outside and was pleased to see the water butt was full.

'Shall I help you tie that up?' asked Jack, making her jump.

'Are you still spying on me?' asked Lizzie stretching to push back a bamboo pole in the ground. At that moment a tarpaulin blew off the log pile and billowed up like the sails of a large ship. Together Jack and Lizzie battled in the heavy rain to capture the run-away tarpaulin and then to anchor it down over the logs to keep them dry for winter burning.

'Thanks,' said Lizzie catching her breath. 'I don't know if I could have managed that on my own.'

'I'm sure you would have managed,' said Jack quietly.

They were sheltering from the heavy rain in her kitchen. The air was filled with the warm and comforting smell of homemade vegetable soup and the crusty loaf that Sally had bought, was sitting on the wooden table waiting to be cut.

'Smells good,' said Jack, but without lifting his eyes. 'Enjoy your meal.' He said as he made to leave by the back door.

'You could join me,' said Lizzie feeling guilty that she'd been so rude to him lately. 'Take it as repayment for your services.'

'Wouldn't that be considered as eating with the enemy?' he said sadly and left without waiting for reply.

Lizzie called after him, 'You know

where I am if you change your mind.' The door closed and Lizzie was left listening to the rain beating on the window pane.

It was a little while before Lizzie had hung up all her wet things and dried her hair. The rain had eased a little and she was just thinking about having her supper and having a go at knitting some gloves for Fiona for Christmas. She would be using the wool that had been sitting in her sewing basket for years rather than the goat hair she'd had little success in spinning.

It was only because the rain had subsided a little that she heard the gentle knock on the door.

'Hello?' Jack stood on the doorstep with his waterproof over his head. In one hand he carried a bottle of red wine and in the other, a small bunch of Michaelmas daisies.

'I won't be upset if you press the flowers to make a picture and use the wine bottle for a flower arrangement, but let's drink the wine first, together?'

'You're lucky, I haven't put the soup on yet.'

'Please take this as a peace offering. I'll be honest with you, Paul did ask me to keep an eye on you, and I agreed. But not as a spy. It's because I care what happens to you.'

7

'Do you think your troublesome goats would eat the remains of the leeks?' asked Jack.

'Yes, they'll love them,' answered Lizzie without looking up from peeling apples.

'That smells good,' said a third voice followed immediately by the flash of a photographer's camera.

'Who are you?' asked Lizzie blinded by the flash.

'Dave, the photographer. We've met before.' He shook hands with Jack and then Lizzie. 'So, what's cooking?'

'Jerusalem artichoke soup,' said Lizzie, leaving the apples and giving the soup a stir.

'It's delicious. I'd never tried them before, but I'm hooked,' said Jack enthusiastically.

'Shall I just put 'making soup' as a

caption?' asked Dave.

'You can put whatever you like, but next time I'd be grateful if you'd knock, rather than just barging in,' said Lizzie in her teacher's voice.

'What? And give you time to hide the TV? I don't think so.'

'There's just no trust, is there?' said Lizzie. 'Now is there anything else you need or are you just leaving?'

'If you're not inviting me to try your soup, then I must be leaving . . . ' said Dave with a smile.

'Goodbye,' said Lizzie concentrating on her apples again and seething. To Jack she said, 'I have to keep reminding myself it's all in a good cause, because otherwise it wouldn't be bearable.'

'It's not that bad surely?' asked Jack coming to sit with her at the kitchen table. 'We've had quite a few laughs.'

Lizzie's first thought was that it was certainly a lot more fun with someone to share it with, but reminded herself, he was just there to spy on her.

'Have you finished with the leeks?' she asked.

'It'll take me one moment to tidy up and feed the bits to the goats. Then what did you want me to do?'

Lizzie was surprised. 'You don't have to do anything,' she snapped and regretted it. 'I'm sorry. I'm used to living on my own going from day to day without seeing many people, and although I do miss company sometimes, I'd got quite used to just my own company and that of the animals.'

'Now, well, you're in and out. There's always workmen and delivery vans next door, people wander up the path to have a look and to top it all photographers burst in uninvited and snap away. I'm fed up with it all and there's months to go.'

Jack had stood up from his seat at the table to go and finish off outside, now he leant forward and gently lay a hand on Lizzie's shoulder.

'Leave me alone!' she snapped feeling

that he was responsible for the work-men and delivery vans and also for spying on her and being in league with Paul and probably his photographer too.

'I'm sorry. I didn't realise you felt like that. The builders are getting to me too, that's one reason why I take refuge here. I didn't realise I wasn't wel-come . . . ' He turned to go and, as he made for the door, he gathered up a few of his belongings that had come with him. His head hung low and Lizzie knew she'd hurt him.

But, thought Lizzie, it's all his fault and I'm hurt too! She listened as he closed the kitchen door and disap-peared. As she came to her senses, she felt guilty because he had helped, even if he did have an ulterior motive. The deal had been that family could help, but anyone else had to be paid.

Lizzie cut the crusty loaf from Sally and served two bowls of soup. She put Jack's on a tray and took it next door to pay her debt.

'Sorry, love, he's gone,' said Joe the builder.

'Gone? But he was here a minute ago,' said Lizzie in surprise.

'He just took a few bits and said he was off and I was to lock up when I've finished.'

'That sounds as though he won't be back this afternoon. Did he say where he was going?' she asked.

'He didn't say anything much. Seemed in a bit of a hurry if you ask me.'

'Thanks anyway,' said Lizzie taking the tray back to her own home.

The next few days were very quiet. Even Joe the builder wasn't around.

Lizzie got back into her old routine, although there was still the nagging thought at the back of her mind that if this crop failed or if something major happened to the house she would struggle, under the terms of their agreement, to put things right.

Richard had taken Sally and the children to EuroDisney for a family break, which they all needed. Fiona had not experienced any more stomach aches. She was just dealing with the side effects of the steroids, but that was a short-term nuisance.

Lizzie had only been writing her piece for a few weeks when she started to be approached by various companies. Garden centres wanted her to mention their name or use their seeds. She was offered goat milking machinery to test out.

Every six weeks or so Lizzie had to check the goats' feet. Being mountain goats they would naturally wear down their toenails, but spending most of their time grazing in a field, sometimes their toenails grew too much and could cause in-growing toenails and cause pain.

This would also mean vet's fees which hadn't been budgeted for.

Lizzie had a collection of concrete slabs in the pen where the goats lived and they would climb on them as they liked to be up high able to see around.

Lizzie managed to get hold of McGinty. She was always easier to catch as Lizzie milked her twice a day. Lizzie sighed when she saw her cloven hoof and that the nails had grown quite a bit since she had last cut them. She was off guard and wished that Jack were around to help.

Quickly she checked herself and reminded herself that she used to be able to find someone to hold the goat while she cut. Usually Richard helped out or sometimes Mr Marshall the farmer. Today, not even the builders were around and could spend ten minutes to help.

Talking quietly and soothingly to McGinty she tried to hold her still and cut her toenails. It wasn't too bad at first, but after a while McGinty wanted to move off and graze and Paddy had come to show an interest in what was going on. He kept nibbling at Lizzie asking for some attention too.

'Be careful!' said Lizzie. 'I don't want to stab you with the cutters,' she told

Paddy, but of course he didn't understand and kept on prodding her so she would respond and tickle his chin and forehead.

Lizzie tried once more but then had to give up for fear of hurting one of the animals if they moved when she wasn't expecting them to.

Instead she decided, as it was getting colder, she would go and look for sticks and logs to burn.

She wasn't out very long, as she couldn't carry very much. As she struggled home with a few logs she wondered if she could construct some form of trailer that she could load up with logs and then drag along.

She was surprised to find a marrow on her doorstep when she got home.

There was no note or explanation and she couldn't think who it could be from.

Instinctively she looked in the windows next door, but it was unoccupied. For the first time Lizzie felt not only alone, but actually lonely. She shivered, the weather was definitely getting cooler, she pulled herself together and tried to convince herself that it was just because Richard and his family were away that she felt on her own, rather than actually missing Jack too. She told herself she should be pleased as she could relax a bit more without him to spy on her.

Lizzie found it easier each week to write up her diary. She thanked the anonymous person who left the marrow, she made light of how hard it was to give the goats a pedicure on her own and how she was just beginning to get a bit fed up of living on fruit and vegetables.

Paul, the editor, had still not really got used to the idea that she had to handwrite her script. He had accepted that she did not have a computer, but did not see why she couldn't go to her local library and use their computers and email it to him from there.

'Hello!' said the postman a few days later. 'I enjoyed your article last week. I could just picture you trying to hold one goat and trim the other one!' He laughed and Lizzie laughed with him, although it was a serious matter. 'Just two postcards today,' he said. 'No fanmail or marrows by post!'

'Thanks,' said Lizzie taking the postcards from him. The first inevitably was from EuroDisney where her brother and his family were having a great time. She knew she would look forward to seeing the photographs.

The second postcard had been sent a few days ago and was also from Paris. Lizzie read it and then re-read it a couple of times. It was from Jack. He was staying just outside Paris. He gave her a phone number and said if she could get someone to goat-and-chicken sit for a few days she should call him and he'll meet her at the airport!

Lizzie was filled with mixed emotions. She was cross that he thought she would drop everything and fly over to be with him and, somehow pleased at the same time that he had even asked her to join him.

A voice interrupted her thoughts. It was Brian Potter, one of the lads she used to teach. He'd last been around when she, Jack and Sidney had shared their fire outside.

'Hello Brian. How are you?'

'I'm fine, Miss,' he said propping his bike up against her fence. 'My mum sent me over.' He counted on his fingers the messages he had to give. 'Mum says she enjoys what you write and can she bring my brother's little girl over to see the goats some time?' He hardly paused for an answer, before he went on to the next part of the message. 'She says I can take you back for Sunday lunch, as she always cooks loads, and Dad's got lots of logs because we've had to take down a tree that's been in the way.' He looked up holding his four fingers behind his back.

'Of course she can bring your niece over and actually, I would really love to come over for Sunday lunch. It's so kind of her to ask. My family are all away, so that would be great.'

'Logs?' said Brian to remind her.

'Haven't you got any use for them?' she asked.

'We've got radiators. Mum says the logs are in the way. She'd be glad to get rid of them.'

'In that case, yes please to the logs and to lunch. When do you eat?'

Brian looked at his watch. 'We usually have a late lunch on a Sunday, about three. Do you remember where I live?' he asked.

'You're the one on the end aren't you?' said Lizzie.

'That's right, number sixteen.'

'I'll walk over about three then. I'm afraid I won't be able to carry many logs home.'

'Don't worry, I'm sure dad will give you a lift home in the van and drop the logs off at the same time.'

'That would be really kind. Thanks Brian and thank your mum for me. I'll see you later,' she called as he cycled off.

Lizzie re-read her postcards again

and set them on the mantelpiece. What with them and Brian's invitation, she didn't feel quite so alone.

Lizzie picked some Michaelmas daisies and a few late roses and tied them up in a bunch for Brian's mum as a thank you.

Carefully she walked round the house checking everything was safely locked up and that the chickens were put away and had fresh water and that the goats were also catered for. She left in good time for the walk to Brian's house. As she walked along she felt herself looking at the hedgerows in a different way. She wasn't just casually aware of the gradual change from summer to autumn, but now she was specifically looking for what she could eat, or use in some way.

She passed a holly tree and made a mental note of that, because time would fly by and Christmas would soon be on its way and she would want to decorate her home with holly and ivy, and anything else in flower or interesting at the time.

8

It was the first week in December. The mornings were cold but crisp and clear, with beautiful bright blue skies. Lizzie's garden was looking a bit bare. Most of her crops had been harvested and were stored either in the shed or the freezer.

There were still leeks in the garden but the recent frost had seen the last of the spinach.

Lizzie sat making Christmas presents for her family. She had warned them all that it was going to be a very simple Christmas this year, and had been delighted that they had decided to join her and make things too.

'Hello!' called a voice from outside, followed by a knock on the door. Lizzie put away her knitting and went to answer the door.

'Hello, Sally, come in,' said Lizzie

standing back to let her sister-in-law enter.

'I can't stay long. I'm helping at school a bit later, but I just wanted to let you know we've had another huge donation for the parents' room — at this rate, we could have a sunken hot tub and cocktail bar as well as a kitchen and sitting-room!'

'That's great!' agreed Lizzie, as she looked at the accounts sheet Sally showed her.

'I'm hoping to have time to pay in a few more cheques before I have to collect Fiona.'

'How's she doing now? She looked a lot happier last weekend.'

'We go back to the hospital next week, and by that time she should have been weaned off the steroids. She'll be really pleased when she feels fit again.' Sally paused. 'By the way, she was wondering if you can come to her nativity play a week Thursday and then the school carol concert on the Friday?'

'I'm sure I'll be able to,' said Lizzie, writing down the dates. As she looked up she caught her sister-in-law looking around.

'You're not spying on me now?' said Lizzie with a deep sigh.

'I haven't seen your spy around lately. Where is he?' asked Sally knowing that Sidney missed him as well as Lizzie.

'Still in Paris, as far as I know.' She tried not to sound too interested.

'I could feed the goats and things if you wanted,' said Sally reluctantly. 'You'd have to show me EXACTLY what to do, and it would be best if Richard and Fiona were here too, but together I'm sure we could hold the fort so you could go to see him.'

Lizzie gave her a hug knowing that looking after smelly goats and chickens was the last thing Sally would ever want to do.

'I do appreciate the offer, but I really don't know if he's still in the same place. It was ages ago when I heard from him. It was when you were away in EuroDisney.'

'Haven't you even phoned him?' asked Sally in surprise as Lizzie shook her head.

'We didn't really hit it off,' said Lizzie rather sadly.

'Nonsense!' said Sally. 'You two made a great pair and he obviously thinks so, otherwise he wouldn't have asked you to join him.'

'We had a bit of an argument,' admitted Lizzie. 'Well, it wasn't even that. I just felt cross because he was spying on me rather than being open and honest and the builders were hammering day in day out but they've more or less finished now. It looks fabulous. I took Joe a cup of tea and some mail for Jack the other day and he showed me round.'

'So, do you think he'll be back for Christmas?' asked Sally. 'If he's going to be on his own, he could join us for Christmas dinner. I hate to think of anyone being on their own.'

'Thanks again, Sally, but I haven't spoken to him, so I really don't know what his plans are.'

'I really thought you two were getting on so well, if you know what I mean. I even thought there might be wedding bells!'

'At my age!' said Lizzie.

'Oh!' said Sally gasping. 'That reminds me, are you going to be in on Wednesday?'

'It's my birthday, but I hadn't any plans. I think Fiona said she was going to come round with a birthday cake for me.'

'She's going to make it herself on Tuesday evening after Brownies. It's all planned, but I do need to be here on Wednesday all day.'

'I'll be here. If it's dry I was planning to mend the netting on the fruit cage,' said Lizzie wondering what Sally was up to.

'I must be off now, but we'll see you after school on Wednesday. Bye,' said Sally, waving as she pulled her coat around her and walked off down the path.

Lizzie made herself a cup of tea with tea bags Sally had given her last time she'd baby-sat. Sally had also made sure the mobile phone had been topped up.

A voice inside Lizzie's head seemed to be saying, 'phone him'. She had been tempted once or twice before, but had always talked herself out of it, but this time she looked at the postcard and dialled the number wondering who would answer.

Just as she dialled the last digit, she paused and rehearsed what she'd say if some woman answered. For all she knew Jack could be married or have a lover.

His invitation may have just been a friendly gesture to give her a break.

After a few sips of tea and a few more deep sighs she dialled the whole number and within seconds she could hear Jack's voice.

'I was just thinking of you,' he said as though he'd never been away. 'I'd made some damson wine when I first came over here and yesterday I was bottling it and I thought I'd give you a bottle for Christmas.'

'Are you coming home?' Lizzie asked. 'Joe says he's more or less finished. It looks great. I hope you don't mind, he showed me round.'

'Of course I don't mind. He has emailed me photos.' There was a slight pause. 'Would I be welcome if I came back?'

Lizzie was glad he couldn't see as she blushed. 'I am sorry. I didn't mean to be so rude, I just didn't feel trusted and that . . . ' she hesitated. 'That hurt.'

'Look, this must be costing a fortune. I'll be in touch.' He said and the phone went dead.

Lizzie stared at the mobile and realised she still knew very little about Jack Curtis.

There was still tea in the pot so she poured two mugs and went next door to where Joe was putting the finishing touches on the kitchen.

'Tell me everything you know about

Jack Curtis,' she demanded.

An hour later Lizzie left with two empty cups and a lot to think about.

Lizzie loved this time of year because the garden always looked so neat and tidy. She had dug over all the beds, mended fences and cut back bushes. She found it satisfying to lean back on her fork and survey her land.

'Hi, Miss,' said a voice breaking into her thoughts. Brian had become a regular visitor and had even helped hold down Paddy while Lizzie checked whether his nails needed trimming or not.

'Hello again,' greeted Lizzie. 'Twice this week!' she said.

'Can't stop long today,' he said. 'Just wanted to drop these round.' He held up a string bag of satsumas. 'Don't say no, it's a thank you for signing my passport form.'

'Thank you,' said Lizzie gratefully accepting the fruit. 'I shall really look forward to these.' She breathed in their citrus smell. 'Have you posted everything off now?'

'Just done it. I can't wait. I should've done it years ago.' Brian looked down at his feet. 'Thanks,' he said quietly.

'For nagging you?' Lizzie laughed. 'Just make sure you come to see me when you and Lee get back and tell me all about it.'

'You bet!' said Brian as he made his way off.

'Thanks for the fruit!' Lizzie called and watched him disappear into the distance before venturing inside for a hot drink.

The kettle boiled and she made the tea, but while it was brewing she succumbed to a second piece of fruit. As she peeled this one she heard the rumble of a delivery van struggling up the grass path. She sighed. It had probably been over a month since Jack had had his last delivery next door and that was one thing she had not missed.

There followed a loud knock at the door. Lizzie assumed Joe wasn't next door and she would have to sign for something for Jack. At least, she thought that would give her another excuse to contact him.

'Miss Elliot?' said the driver.

Lizzie nodded but said, 'I'm not expecting anything.'

'Deluxe duck house, it says here,' he told her. 'Ordered by a Mrs Elliot.'

The strange conversation with Sally filtered back to her, but a duck house! What would she want with a duck house? Although, no doubt it would be a lot smarter than her old chicken coop which she'd bought second-hand from someone in the next village.

'Where shall I put it?' asked the driver giving her a clipboard to sign for the delivery.

'It's on wheels. So, shall I put it in the front and you can move it around to where you want it.'

'Thank you,' said Lizzie, feeling a bit bemused.

It was a very grand duck house suitable for three or four ducks. Lizzie had mentioned some time ago, when she had watched the film, *Babe*, with Fiona and Sidney that she loved the comic way Ferdinand the Indian Runner Duck waddled and that if she ever kept ducks, that would be the sort she'd have, but she didn't have a pond!

Lizzie had a productive afternoon. She finished off the fingerless gloves she'd been knitting for Fiona. They hadn't been nearly so fiddly as the ones she'd done for Sidney who still had such tiny fingers.

She tied a pretty bow around the lid of the Kilner Jar which she'd filled with pears from her pear tree, in brandy. Over the years Lizzie had acquired an odd collection of alcoholic drinks that people had given her as gifts for various things and this year had seemed the right time to use some of these spirits.

Lizzie thought Sally might enjoy the pears for a dinner party dessert. Lizzie had also made a rum pot and now decanted the raspberries from her garden, steeped in rum and put them in another jar as another gift for Sally and another for a friend.

Lizzie was just clearing up when she heard voices coming up the path and guessed it was Sally with the children. Quickly she hid the Christmas presents and went to the door to greet her family.

Fiona carried a tin very carefully and even Sidney was laden down with bags.

'It arrived then?' said Sally acknowledging the duck house. Lizzie didn't really know what to say, so she just gave Sally a big hug and both wiped away a tear.

Lizzie recalled her previous birthday. Sally had given her a beautiful basket of lavender products for her bathroom. It had obviously been expensive and the basket matched others she had in her bathroom, but it had seemed to Lizzie as though Sally felt that living at Milkmaid's Cottage was somehow dirty.

However, this year, not just on her birthday, but for some months now,

Sally had become much more in tune with Lizzie and with her chosen life.

The kitchen was full of activity. Fiona proudly showed off the cake she'd made. It looked more like an Easter Cake than a birthday cake because of the ducks.

'You've no idea how difficult it was to get ducks at this time of year,' Sally was saying. Fiona positioned a token amount of candles and told everyone to stand back while she lit them.

There was a faint knock just audible above the enthusiastic singing of 'Happy Birthday'. Jack popped his head round the door with a huge hand tied bouquet of flowers and holding a bottle of wine.

'Sorry, have I called at a bad time?' he said and immediately withdrew. 'Don't worry, I'll call back later.'

'Nonsense!' said Sally almost dragging him in. 'You must have a bit of birthday cake.'

Fiona helped Sally as they unpacked a picnic hamper full of food for the special birthday tea.

'You must think I don't eat,' said Lizzie watching as yet another plate of sandwiches appeared. 'Can I help?'

'No. You just sit and enjoy being waited on,' Sally told her and then said. 'Why don't you go and show Jack the duck house before it's too dark and we'll get tea ready. I'll get Sidney to come and fetch you when we're ready.'

Lizzie did as she was told and took Jack back outside to inspect her present.

'Have you got ducks?' asked Jack.

'No,' admitted Lizzie quietly. 'It's something I've considered . . . '

'They make excellent guard dogs,' Jack told her with enthusiasm. 'We have some in France.'

'Don't you mean geese?' asked Lizzie and Jack laughed.

'I know I've got a great deal to learn about the countryside, but I do know the difference between a duck and a goose. And I don't just mean the taste!'

'I'm sorry,' said Lizzie feeling embarrassed. 'I didn't mean . . . ' she stumbled for words. She wanted the ground to open up and swallow her. Jack had walked back into her life looking even more handsome than she'd remembered and set her heart fluttering and already she'd insulted him. 'I just thought it was geese that were used as guard dogs,' she said humbly. 'My mistake.'

'Do you want ducks?' asked Jack ignoring what she'd said and inspecting the duck house with interest.

'I suppose so,' said Lizzie. 'I was thinking this afternoon that I ought to go to the library to do some research.'

'Ah ha!' said Jack with a smile. 'At last! Something that I may be able to help you with.' Lizzie didn't know what to say but got the distinct impression that she'd come across as an expert at living off the land and had somehow, unwittingly undermined him.

'Do you know about ducks?' she asked.

'I've kept them for years,' he told her. 'Of course, those were French ducks, but I do know a good supplier near here. It was something I had hoped to have when I bought the cottage, but . . . well, then I didn't think it was meant to be.'

'Joe's done a really good job,' said Lizzie looking up at his house.

'I'll have to go and inspect,' said Jack. 'We could go in now, if you like?' he asked.

'Haven't you been in yet?' asked Lizzie wide-eyed and incredulous. Jack hung his head.

'No. I came straight over to see you,' he said quietly. 'I missed you.'

Lizzie thought she heard what he'd said and was about to admit she'd missed him, more than she had ever missed anyone, but at that moment Sidney came rushing out into the garden calling them back in for tea.

'Don't worry,' said Lizzie later. 'I'll clear away,' she told Sally as she stroked Sidney's forehead. He was sleepy and even Fiona had hidden a yawn.

'Don't worry,' Jack echoed. 'I'll help her.'

'Well, that would be great,' agreed Sally. 'Now, don't forget, both of you, school nativity on Thursday and carol concert on Friday.'

'Bye!' called Jack and Lizzie together. They paused for a moment and looked at each other, then responded to Fiona's calls and waved goodbye.

Jack shut the door and took Lizzie in his arms. He held her close. She could feel all sorts of things.

Lizzie was aware of Jack tenderly kissing the top of her hair and stroking her back. It was a moment that had taken her by surprise and she wasn't ready for it.

His hug seemed to last forever and yet in a moment it was over and he was looking a bit embarrassed. Lizzie stumbled as she regained her balance. He steadied her and she wanted him to hold her again, but Jack was heading for the kitchen to clear up the remains of tea.

'I'd put those in water if I were you,' said Jack pointing to the beautiful flowers he'd bought her.

'Thank you,' she said smelling the creamy roses and lilies. They were tied with dark green leaves and the contrast was beautiful.

As they washed up and put everything away, they made small talk. Lizzie couldn't help thinking how natural the situation seemed. She found herself looking at Jack in a different way. She studied the back of his head, the line of his shoulders, and the muscles on his strong arms.

'Oh!' she exclaimed as she picked up the bottle of wine he'd bought. 'Your damson wine, I thought that was meant to be a Christmas present.'

Jack turned and gave her a heart-melting smile, but Lizzie gasped and then coughed, as she couldn't get her breath.

'What's wrong?' he asked.

There was no way Lizzie could admit it was a horrible thought she'd just had.

'Are you staying, or going back to France?' she blurted out. 'For Christmas, I mean.'

'That depends on you,' he said mysteriously. 'But now I've got commitments until at least Friday, what with the nativity and the carol concert and . . . ' he reached into his jacket pocket which was on the back of one of the kitchen chairs. He pulled out a couple of tickets. 'Are you busy on Saturday?' he asked.

'I've no plans for Saturday,' admitted Lizzie feeling strangely excited.

'These were on sale in the florist where I got your flowers.' He showed her the tickets. They were for the local Christmas Barn Dance on the farm. 'Would you be my guest?'

9

Sidney insisted, ignoring Sally's protests, on sitting on Jack's lap during the nativity. Fiona was an angel. At first she hid at the back of the angelic choir, but gradually her confidence increased and she smiled and waved at them all.

Richard made it home for the carol concert on Friday. Sidney was so excited, he didn't know where he wanted to sit. In fact they were lucky to get a seat at all and were squashed together in the school hall.

Lizzie was all too aware of being so close to Jack. He had awakened feelings in her in the last week that she hadn't even known she had inside her.

Jack walked Lizzie home that evening after sharing a Christmas drink with Sally and Richard. They walked along in companionable silence. Her arm touching his every so often as they strolled along in time with each other.

As they reached the lane that led up to the cottages, Jack felt for her hand and entwined his fingers in hers. It was a protective gesture but nothing more was said until they reached Lizzie's gate.

'I could take you to the duck place in the morning if you like,' offered Jack.

'Thank you,' said Lizzie.

They agreed a time and before she knew it, he'd left her side and was heading off next door to his own place. 'Do you fancy coming in for a coffee?' called Lizzie.

'I can't tonight, I'm afraid,' he said and sadly she watched him go.

To Lizzie it felt doubly cruel having him so close and yet so far away. She could not get him out of her mind. She could smell his aftershave. She could picture him standing at the sink helping her clear up after her birthday party.

She had a fretful night. Visions of Jack kept coming in and out of her dreams and her waking thoughts. At about 4 a.m. she got up unable to sleep and made herself a cup of tea.

Lizzie sat at her kitchen table wrapped up in a thick towelling dressing gown. She stared at the empty cup and sighed. She had thought her life was complete. She'd had an enjoyable career, earned good money, travelled all over the world, had her own home the way she wanted it and now was content to live very simply feeling she was closer to nature and more peaceful.

That was, until Jack had come into her life and turned everything upside-down! Now she was questioning her very existence.

This evening had shocked her. She had assumed, wrongly, that he would have come in and spent the evening with her. Lizzie had got used to his company. Since he'd returned from France they had spent nearly all their time together. It had felt so right and natural as if he had never been away, but now . . . now she felt so lonely and empty.

Lizzie told herself she would have to get used to the feeling. 'I'm not a teenager,' she told herself. 'This is stupid, getting so involved with him.'

This evening, when he reached for her hand, it had probably only been to steady her as they walked along the uneven path.

The sound of a car outside interrupted her thoughts. They didn't get much traffic during the day, let alone in the early hours in the morning.

Lizzie pulled her dressing gown around her and went to the front room to see what it was. She didn't want to draw attention to herself, and so left the light off.

To her amazement it was the familiar Jaguar driven by Paul. He dropped Jack off and then, a bit too noisily, reversed back down the track to the main road. As Jack switched on his house lights it confirmed the red colour of the Jag. There was no mistaking who it belonged to.

She knew it was none of her business,

but nevertheless she could not help wondering why they were out together until the early hours of the morning. What did they have to say to each other? What were they up to? Why did it concern her that Jack was speaking to that awful man from the newspaper? She knew they were related, but they seemed so very different.

She finished her tea and stormed upstairs to bed in an effort to rid herself of the mixture of feelings that now ebbed and flowed through her body.

She'd just got settled in bed and warm again when she was sure she heard a knock at the door. Checking the clock, she realised it was just gone 5 a.m. She suspected it was Jack but didn't trust herself to go and see for herself. She was so cross with him, but also knew that if he'd taken her into his arms again . . . she didn't know what would happen.

She had never felt so strongly about someone for a long time. The feelings surprised her and scared her. After all these years of being alone, she was finding it hard to come to terms with these dormant feelings rising up and wasn't really sure how to handle them.

The following morning Lizzie found a note that had been pushed through her letterbox. It was from Jack apologising that he could no longer make their morning trip to the duck farm, but he would be able to take her later on in the day before the barn dance in the evening.

Lizzie fumed. She suspected he would be sleeping in after his very late night out with the distasteful Paul. She paced up and down, wondering what to do with her morning. She had slept deeply and although it had taken her a while to initially get off, she felt rested.

Lizzie put on her winter coat and grabbed her flower scissors. She'd already seen to the animals and had her breakfast. She marched off in search of holly and ivy and anything else that would cheer up her home and make it look Christmassy.

The fresh air and her sense of purpose made her feel a lot happier. She paused when she saw a ball of mistletoe in a tree and decided to leave it where it was.

On arriving home, she found some-one had left a box of things for her. She suspected it was probably Brian Potter or his mum. The box contained nuts and satsumas and home-made WI chutney and a jar of pickled onions.

She glanced around to see if there was anyone around to thank, but there was not a soul in sight. She couldn't help noticing how unlived in Mulberry Cottage looked. Jack had not got around to buying any curtains or soft furnishings. His house looked quite bare, it was not yet a home.

Lizzie had originally thought she would offer to take Jack shopping for curtains etc., once they'd visited the duck farm, but now she wasn't really sure what she wanted to do.

However, the moment she saw Jack Curtis stroll up the path to meet her, all her thoughts turned to jelly and she couldn't string a sentence together without tripping up over the words.

Mrs Wilson lived in an end of terrace house. The house itself was nothing special to look at, but the back garden was a haven for ducks. Interestingly she had no large pond, but several decent-sized puddles where the ducks wadded in and used their beaks to search for insects and probably frogs.

'The ideal place would be in that boggy piece of land in the top left-hand part of my garden,' said Jack taking the thoughts right out of Lizzie's mind. 'We could put a really sturdy fence round both the cottages and that would help deter the foxes. We could have a gate into the goat field . . . '

'You've got it all worked out,' said Lizzie with a smile.

'I had a lot of time to think when I was in France. Sometime I'll show you my plans,' he said and Lizzie couldn't help wondering what, in particular he'd been thinking about in France. 'Surely he wasn't just after her property?'

They chose one male and two female ducks and agreed to collect them when they'd got themselves organised at home. Lizzie was aware that throughout the conversation with Mrs Wilson, it appeared that they were an item buying the ducks for their freehold.

'I bet you're thinking of names,' said Jack as they drove away.

'No, I'll leave it to Fiona and Sidney to name them, although I bet the male will be Donald!' said Lizzie feeling at ease and relaxed. She realised, rather uncomfortably, she was happier in Jack's company and was miserable without him. 'I wondered if you wanted me to show you some places to get soft furnishings?'

'How can furniture be soft?' asked Jack.

'Don't be silly,' she teased. 'Curtains, rugs, cushions, that sort of thing.'

'I'm not really interested in all that at the moment,' he said.

'But . . . ' began Lizzie. She stopped

and accepted that it was his house and if he wanted it cold and bare, then it was up to him. 'Perhaps you'd drop me at Richard's?' she asked.

Jack looked surprised but didn't say anything. He kept the engine running as she got out to show he had no intention of coming in, maybe he felt he needed an invitation, but if that was the case he'd only need to wait until she'd knocked at the door. But he didn't wait.

Fiona was now off the steroids, which she was really happy about. She still had to take other tablets to keep the ulcers at bay, but it was the steroids that had the unpleasant side effect and the extra weight gain had knocked her confidence.

'How do you keep fit, Auntie Liz?' asked Fiona.

'I work out at the green gym every day,' Lizzie told her. Fiona gave her a disbelieving look. 'My garden keeps me fit. I do weight lifting when I carry the goat mix in, that's a 25kg bag. I exercise all sorts of different muscles when I dig. I stretch up to pick apples and pears and I need to be supple to pick raspberries and collect the eggs.'

'Mummy and I have been swimming every day this week!'

'That's good exercise too,' agreed Lizzie. 'I'm going to a barn dance tonight, and that's exercise too, but great fun.' Lizzie didn't know why she'd said it, but for some reason she felt compelled to bring Jack into the conversation.

'What are you going to wear?' asked Sally entering the room and catching the piece of conversation about the barn dance.

'I've got a pair of jeans and a checked blouse. I wondered about a necktie?'

'Had you thought of the feminine touch? Maybe a flowing skirt? I could lend you one, if you like.' Sally didn't wait for an answer but disappeared up the stairs to fetch the skirt she had been talking about.

The vast majority of people were

dressed in jeans but Lizzie felt comfortable in her borrowed denim skirt, blue and grey checked blouse and suede boots. Left to her own devices she had to admit to Sally she'd probably have ended up wearing Wellingtons and they would not be comfy to dance in all evening.

Jack wore jeans and a dark blue shirt, the colour of which brought out the blue in his eyes and Lizzie thought he looked more dashing than ever.

He offered her his hand for the first dance and it was as if an electric shock went through his body and into hers as he led her on to the dance floor and then stood close beside her in a square dance.

The Caller was excellent and got a real banter going with the dancers. He soon picked up on the fact that whenever he looked, Lizzie and Jack were holding hands, even when they shouldn't have been.

They danced about four dances in a row and then stepped out of the barn for a bit of cooler night air.

Lizzie had never felt so alive. Her senses seemed heightened and she was suddenly aware of every smell from the barbeque, the familiar smell of Jack's aftershave, the warm, sweet smell of the straw in the barn.

Jack pulled her gently to face him. He held her at arms length, placing his hands on her shoulders. Gently he placed a finger under her chin and raised her face to his. She expected a kiss but instead he was looking at her with a sad and serious face. Suddenly she was filled with fear that he was going away again.

'Why didn't you come and meet Teresa?' he asked.

'Teresa?' asked Lizzie feeling as though she'd been slapped round the face. He spoke her name so tenderly and Lizzie had to admit she was jealous. She didn't even know who this woman was, but Jack obviously cared about her.

'In France,' said Jack as though that

would explain everything.

'What are you talking about? I got one postcard with your phone number asking me to join you in France. I have goats and chickens to feed and, well, I hardly knew, know you,' corrected Lizzie.

'And the texts and the messages. You never even replied and I needed you with me. It would have made it so much better.'

'What are you talking about?' asked Lizzie stepping back and away from him. He seemed to be accusing her of something and she genuinely had no idea what he was talking about.

'Teresa was dying, I really wanted you to meet her before it was too late. It would have meant a lot to me and to her too. I do wish you'd come.'

'I'm sorry Jack, you'll have to rewind and fill in all the gaps. All I had was one postcard and, as I said, I hardly know you, or knew you then and . . . '

'Didn't you get the messages from Paul?'

Lizzie shook her head. 'Or the texts?' Lizzie threw up her hands. 'That may be my fault, I'm a complete novice with the mobile phone. I answer if it rings and the only call I've made, I think, was to you in France. I see it just as a tool for Sally to contact me if Fiona's taken ill again.'

'Oh,' said Jack quietly. They stood in silence for a while. She wanted to be forgiven and held close in his arms.

'So, who is Teresa?' asked Lizzie not really wanting to know, but knowing she needed to settle this matter.

'Come and sit down,' said Jack leading her to a straw bale. 'It's a long story. I assumed you knew about it, but I can see I was wrong.'

Lizzie sat down beside him on the straw bale. He put an arm around her and checked that she was comfortable and not too cold.

'Years ago,' he swallowed, finding the words hard to say, 'I was to be married. We'd bought Mulberry Cottage with the idea that one day we would also buy

Milkmaid's Cottage and knock the two together when we had a family. We were young and full of foolish dreams.'

He sighed a deep, deep sigh and then continued. 'One evening we'd dropped a few things off at the cottage. It was the eve of our wedding but the place wasn't really fit to live in, as you said the other day, it was a house but not a home. We'd had a bit of an argument. It was all my fault, I'm ashamed to say I wanted us to spend the night at the cottage but she wouldn't have any of it. She stormed out and, that was the last I saw of her. There was a car crash. I don't know if I caused it. If she was in tears or driving too fast because she was angry or . . .'

Lizzie squeezed his hand and looked up at him but Jack turned away. It only lasted a moment, before he resumed his story. 'Looking back I realised we'd had a lot of little arguments lately. I'd put it down to the stress of the wedding, but now I can see that we weren't really right for each other. Most of the wedding guests stayed for the funeral and, as you can imagine, it was an awful time.'

'I should have stayed and supported my family, but I just had to get away. A job came up in France and I took it. I stayed with an old French couple, Philippe and Teresa. They'd never had a family and they 'adopted' me. I started a new life and put the past behind me. Then Philippe died and I wondered about bringing Teresa over here and looking after her. The French house was stone and always cold, but I suppose we were used to it.'

'Is that why you seem so reluctant to decorate Mulberry Cottage now and make it a home?' asked Lizzie. 'I'm surprised you ever wanted to see the place again.'

'I didn't. I came back to inspect it, get it valued and sell it. But, you were in the garden and you smiled at me, and, well I guess I saw the place differently after that.'

Lizzie had heard what he'd said but she found it hard to take it.

'I asked Joe to help me convert it for Teresa but she'd suddenly deteriorated and that's why I went back to France. I had to be with her, she'd been like a mother to me. I so wanted her to meet you but at least she died knowing that at last I'd found true love, and that made her happy.'

Again, Lizzie had heard what he said, but it all seemed like a story in third person and she couldn't accept that she was one of the characters in the story.

'Are you two coming back to dance?' asked one of the other dancers. 'The Caller's asking for the Lovebirds!'

Jack stood and offered his hand to Lizzie and together they entered the barn. The rest of the evening was a bit of a dream for Lizzie. She danced, every so often they would touch shoulders or hold hands but all the time she could feel Jack's eyes on her. It didn't seem to matter who he was dancing with, she felt he only had eyes for her.

10

It had been a long winter but now spring was on its way. Lizzie got up early and planted peas, beans, new potatoes and had a greenhouse full of seedlings. It was a busy time and a crucial one for the garden.

Lizzie coughed as she collected the duck eggs. Donald, Jemima Puddle Duck and Daphne had settled in well and often brought a smile to her face as they waddled comically about the place.

Jack had been away again. He'd gone back to France to sort out the property and clear up all the loose ends to put a close on that part of his life.

Lizzie coughed again and put her hand to her head. She had woken with a thumping headache which was unlike her. She'd hoped the fresh air would have cleared it, but it lingered.

She chewed on a bit of willow hoping that its medicinal properties would help her. She felt it got her through the morning chores but by lunchtime Lizzie was experiencing hot flushes and cold sweats. She decided to give in and have a nap — just a short one, but later found she had no energy to get out of bed, not even to put the chickens and ducks safely away.

Ironically it was Paul Curtis who first realised something was wrong. For the first time, Lizzie missed the deadline, there was no article from her to fill the gap they had allocated to her and sold advertising to support. The editor had been on to Paul and he had phoned Sally to chase Lizzie up as this was all part of the package.

Sally wasted no time in going over to Lizzie's. She became more anxious as she walked up the lane and was met by two runaway ducks. Sally rang home and explained to Richard that she may need his help.

'Lizzie!' called Sally as she approached,

but received no reply. Sally called again but it was Jack who answered.

'I think she's out,' he called. 'I just popped in a few minutes ago and there was no sign of her.'

'But the ducks are out and . . . the goat bucket has hardly any water, even I know something's not right!' said Sally pleased with herself for noticing these little things.

Jack was over the fence in no time and together they called and crept up the stairs. Sally went first and knocked on Lizzie's bedroom door. Lizzie groaned from within.

'What's wrong?' asked Sally as she stroked her sister-in-law's brow. 'Golly, you're hot!' She tried to pull some covers off Lizzie, but Lizzie snatched them back.

'She's shivering,' said Jack.

'I'll call the doctor,' said Sally going down the stairs.

The doctor diagnosed flu and told Lizzie she just had to rest. Lizzie's fight had gone and she just lay there lacking energy and spirit. She slept and slept while around her Sidney and Fiona fed and watered the goats, collected the eggs and chased the ducks until they were back in their pen.

Jack and Richard sat at the kitchen table and did their best putting a diary piece together but neither really knew what to say.

'Why don't you take some photos?' suggested Fiona and both the men looked at her knowing she'd got them out of a sticky situation. Richard snapped away with his digital camera and Jack noted down captions, then they both went next door to where Jack had a computer and they emailed the pictures to the newspaper.

In the meantime Sally had decided Lizzie's home needed a good spring clean and she had taken down curtains and was busy making a washing pile to take home.

Later Sally took the children and the washing home while Richard cut logs for the fire and Jack did the lawns. On her way home Sally met up with Mrs Marshall from the farm and told her that Lizzie wasn't well. Mrs M insisted Sally should take some homemade broth to Lizzie to try and get her to eat something.

Jack spent that night sitting beside Lizzie as she lay, still sleeping in bed. The following day Sally brought over more food for them both, although Lizzie ate very little.

The whole village now knew of Lizzie's flu and, as rumours have it, it had grown and to some it sounded as though she were on her deathbed with her family all around her.

Gifts poured in from well-wishers and people brought flowers. Jack had to be quick with the flowers because Paddy had a real taste for them.

Inevitably, a reporter arrived and interviewed anyone who would speak to him.

That evening Jack prepared to stay by Lizzie's bedside once again.

'What are you doing?' asked Lizzie as

he made himself comfy in the chair beside her bed.

'I'm afraid I've got a bit of a shock for you!' he said, but with a smile, 'I've been sleeping beside you all week!'

'Oh!' said Lizzie and then she laughed. 'Thank you for looking after me. I'm sure I'd have been fine, but it's good to know you cared enough to stay, unless . . . ' she paused and looked at him seriously, 'Unless you did really think I was going to die and so you could phone that awful Paul and have him send a photographer down to record my dying moments!'

'That awful Paul,' said Jack, 'is my brother!'

'Your brother!' exclaimed Lizzie feeling weak again and sinking down on to the bed.

'Well, half-brother. My mother died when I was young and then, years later, my father remarried and they had Paul and then they died. Paul's OK really, he's just doing his job and he's had a hard life too.'

'I'm sorry. I can't feel sorry for him. He always seems so hard,' said Lizzie clutching the end of the bed.

'He's angry that's all. He married a while back and they were going to live in Mulberry Cottage because I had no use for it, but then his wife left him almost as soon as the honeymoon was over. He's been angry ever since. It just covers up his hurt. Now he's married to his job, but I think he is beginning to soften.'

Lizzie yawned and let Jack help her into bed, within minutes she was fast asleep even though she had slept for most of the day.

Lizzie woke first the following morning and felt so much better. She tiptoed downstairs to make them both a cup of tea.

'Jack?' she called ready to hand him his cup but there was no response. She put down the cups and lent over to kiss him on his forehead. He stirred.

'Now that's the way to be woken in the morning!' he said with a smile.

'You've been busy!' said Lizzie. 'The greenhouse has been mended, the log pile is stacked high, the place looks like it's been cleaned from top to bottom and I haven't lost any animals.'

'There's been a team of us. You won't believe how many people had mucked in and kept things going until you were better. You've got a lot of friends.'

'Are we friends?' asked Lizzie seriously, taking a sip of her tea. Jack pondered on her question.

'Yes,' he said at last.

'You had to think about that,' she queried.

'That's because,' began Jack, 'I'd like to think we were more than just friends.' He paused and looked at her. Lizzie met his gaze and then lowered her lids. 'I do hope you consider me your friend because we can't build a deeper relationship if we're not even friends.'

Lizzie stood and began to gather things to go and wash. 'Where are you going?' asked Jack.

'To wash,' replied Lizzie simply. Jack gently pulled her towards him. He cleared his throat.

'We've established we're friends. You know I care for you. No,' he corrected himself, 'I love you. I've been trying to tell you, but everyone I've ever loved has gone away, and I was scared, and then when you were ill . . . I just need you to know how I feel,' he declared.

This time, Lizzie reached out for his hand. 'I didn't think I'd ever admit this, but I've fallen in love with you too!'

Jack scooped her into his arms and kissed her again and again.

'Will you marry me?'

'Don't ask,' said Lizzie. 'At least don't ask me here.'

'But if I did ask you again . . . '

'You know I love you, Jack, and want to be with you,' said Lizzie.

That afternoon Sally had taken Lizzie out for a short drive. They'd had afternoon tea together and pored over plans for the hospital parents' room.

'We're nearly there,' said Sally. 'I know you did it for Fiona, but thank you. You've given me a new lease of life too.'

When they returned to Milkmaid's Cottage, Jack had been busy. The kitchen table had been laid with a tablecloth and flowers. A bottle of Mrs Marshall's best elderflower champagne was chilling in the fridge and a delicious smell was coming from the stove.

Sally took one look at the table and said, 'I won't stop.' She kissed Lizzie goodbye and winked at Jack.

'Now why don't you go and freshen up, perhaps put on a pretty dress — you've got about ten minutes!'

When Lizzie returned to the kitchen, duly dressed in her one and only dress, she was amazed to see Jack in a dinner jacket and bow tie. There was a vase of red roses on the mantelpiece and music was playing softly.

'Wow!' said Lizzie. 'You have been busy.'

'I've had a bit of help,' admitted Jack. 'It's all home grown and organic, but not necessarily homemade by me. Here, let's toast your good health with a glass of champagne.'

As Lizzie sipped her drink the bubbles tingled in her mouth. She took another sip and was vaguely aware of Jack kneeling on the floor.

'Have you lost something?' she asked innocently. He took her hand and looked up at her from his kneeling position.

'Will you marry me?' he asked again and this time Lizzie agreed.

By the time the year was up and Lizzie had managed to live self-sufficiently, albeit with help from friends and family, Lizzie and Jack had officially announced their engagement.

There had been a front page story with a picture of Lizzie and Paul shaking hands with one hand and Paul handing over the cheque with the other. It had been an honourable wager and Lizzie had won.

'Think of it as a community project,' Sally had told her. 'Besides, Paul will soon be your brother-in-law and it's about time you became friends.'

'I understand him a bit more now I know his story. I was cross with myself for judging him without taking the trouble to get to know him.'

'That's not like you, Lizzie. You always like everyone, but I suppose you were just sticking up for Fiona initially.'

'And look where that's led us!' said Jack snaking an arm around Lizzie. 'I can't believe how lucky I am!'

Work had actually started on the hospital. A kitchen was being fitted for parents to use. An on-going charity fund had been set up to provide tea and coffee for parents as well as bedding and a laundry service so that parents could relax and concentrate on the well-being of their sick child.

Lizzie and Jack had agreed plans with Joe the builder to alter their cottages slightly in order to make the semis into one dwelling.

The other plans were wedding plans. 'Look!' said Jack with a smile.

'There's no way we're going to be able to have a quiet affair.' He showed Lizzie the note attached to a bag of rose petals. It simply said, 'You promised'.

THE END